IRAN + 100

STORIES FROM A CENTURY AFTER THE COUP

EDITED BY
FERESHTEH AHMADI,
PETER ADRIAN BEHRAVESH & REBECCA ZAHABI

First published in Great Britain in 2025 by Comma Press.
www.commapress.co.uk

A CIP catalogue record of this book is available from the British Library.

ISBN-10: 1912697963
ISBN-13: 978-1912697960

This book has been selected to receive financial assistance from
English PEN's 'PEN Translates' programme.

The publisher gratefully acknowledges the support of Arts Council England.

Printed and bound in England by CPI Group (UK) Ltd, Croydon CR0 4YY

Contents

CONTENTS

Foreword

THE PAST 72 YEARS of Middle East history have been marked by upheaval and profound transformation – shaped by geography, by the region's role as a bridge between East and West, by its vast energy resources, by colonialist interests in those resources, and by a rich and ancient culture deeply intertwined with religion. Historians and politicians have offered countless analyses and taken diverse stances on this tumultuous century, but it is often through the lens of artists and writers – free from overt political positions and steeped in metaphor – that overlooked or less visible dimensions emerge.

This anthology attempts to shed light on some of the most important events of the past 72 years and imagine futures shaped by them, through short stories written by authors whose lived experiences are intimately tied to this volatile region.

For Iran in particular, the August 1953 coup that led to the ousting of Prime Minister Mohammad Mosaddegh is considered the starting point of so much of this history. An event that reversed Mosaddegh's apparent plan to nationalise Iran's oil fields, and allowed the monarchy of Mohammad Reza Pahlavi Shah to endure (some would say as a 'puppet' of the Americans and the British) for another 26 years – and one which, according to many, created a deep rift in Iranian society, a fracture that resulted in decades of political unrest, from the protests of 1963[1] to the 'Dah Shab' (Ten Nights) of 1977,[2] culminating in the Islamic Revolution of 1979 but also continuing to reverberate even today, with recent phenomena like the 'Woman, Life, Freedom' protests of 2022.

Some attribute the 1953 coup to an alliance between traditionalist right-wing forces (including the CIA and MI5) and religious groups, while others deny the coup entirely or cast doubt on Mosaddegh's stance. But regardless of these perspectives, it is undeniable that after August 1953, the influence of various ideologies and social classes on Iran's political future became increasingly visible. The traditional right, the merchant class, the religious, the leftists, the workers, and even the emerging urban middle class — described by some as a fragile and delicate layer — would go on to play crucial and active roles in subsequent events, including the 1979 Islamic Revolution.

Following the revolution, the urban middle class, which had grown more prominent and influential over the last seven decades, helping to shape contemporary Iranian art and literature along the way, became more vocal, more engaged. It demanded its rights, took to the streets, challenged dominant societal values. Within this class, women in particular have taken on increasingly active roles over the past 40 years. Despite state repression and censorship, their voices have risen above the silence — resonating loudly and clearly with the world in 2022's women-led uprising.

Given the century under discussion, the year 2053 — our imagined future — no longer feels distant. Yet the pace of change in today's world is so rapid that these writers, whether or not they see that future as near, step boldly into speculative realms, envisioning what Iran might become.

Before we examine the recurring themes in some of these stories, let us briefly consider the history of science fiction in Iran, that is to say, the *literary* context from which they're being written. This offers insight into the legacy and influences that have shaped contemporary Iranian writers working in this genre.

FOREWORD

Long before the modern era, traces of fantastical imagination can be found scattered throughout ancient tales and myths – from *The Epic of Gilgamesh*, the stories in *The Shahnameh*, and *One Thousand and One Nights* – stories that endowed humans with capabilities that, in time, technology would render possible. But it is only in the late 19th century that the concept of the future, divorced from religious notions like the apocalypse, begins to appear and science fiction – as we now understand it – emerges. Abdolhossein Sanatizadeh published the first Persian utopian novel, *The Assembly of Lunatics*, in 1903, followed by *Rostam in the 22nd Century* in 1913 – considered the first Persian science fiction novel. Alongside him, Abdollah Nahid is recognised as another early pioneer, most notably for *How I Went to Mars* (1940), which tells of a spaceship landing in Saqqez and the protagonist's subsequent journey with the Martians.

Yet despite these early examples, the development of science fiction in Persian has largely been shaped by translations. Many original Persian stories closely mirror the structure and themes of Western works – particularly those translated from French and English. Early among them were Mary Shelley's seminal *Frankenstein* and Karel Čapek's *The Absolute at Large*. In the years following the 1953 coup, in part due to America's greater interest in Iran, Western influence deepened, and science fiction gained a larger readership. Nearly all of Jules Verne's novels were translated into Persian, and the desire to foresee the future and fulfil human aspirations found fertile ground.

It is thus no surprise that many modern Iranian works are indebted to their Western predecessors. However, one must also acknowledge the influence of Persian classical literature. Iranian fantasy, deeply rooted in ancient texts and epics written long before the rise of Western structuralism, has been a significant source for the evolution of Iranian science fiction. A more comprehensive study would require revisiting Persian fables and mythologies and exploring how they have shaped modern storytelling. Mohammad Ghassezadeh, in his 2017 book *A Study of Science Fiction Literature*, touches on this point, examining the fantastical worlds of Ferdowsi's epic poem *Shahnameh* (circa 977-1010 AD), Nezami Ganjavi's *Eskandarnameh* (1209), and the philosophical tale *Hayy ibn Yaqzan (Alive, Son of Awake)* by Ibn Tufail (1105-1185) as important and influential predecessors to the genre.

In this anthology, most of the stories depict post-apocalyptic landscapes. It seems that in the writers' imaginations, the accelerating pace of technological domination, the human destruction of nature, and the draining of the world's lifeblood, make even 30 years sufficient for darkness to descend. Yes, darkness is a recurring motif – closely tied to the even greater theme of energy, and its source: oil. Oil – the cause of most of the region's unrest over the past century. And with oil comes the inevitable presence of industrialised nations and their hunger for energy. In this project's historical scope, the role of Britain in Iran's modern political history – particularly in the 1953 coup – is frequently emphasised, along with the United States, of course, which, in the aftermath of World War II, took it upon itself to reshape the world order in its image, and dictate the destinies of many nations, including Iran.

Beyond overtly realistic themes – like Iran's long-standing oil sanctions, foreign interference in domestic affairs, or references to recent events, such as the killings of street protesters – many of these stories employ metaphor and archetype. Understanding these elements can deepen one's grasp of the stories' atmospheres and hidden meanings: the man suspended for years between earth and sky who cannot die, in Navid Hamzavi's story; the time warps in Ebrahim Farrokh's piece; the exhumation of Mosaddegh's body and the attempt to relocate his burial site in Behnam Yousefpour's tale; the walls encircling Iran and a school principal who seeks to return the oil to the earth in Nasim Marashi's narrative; or the putrid, breathing pit that devours everything in 'The Tomb'.

To interpret these, one needs some knowledge of Iran's socio-political history. Yet the good news is that these metaphors also point to larger, more universal archetypes – timeless and unbound by geography. That is what makes them archetypes. Situations such as being trapped in an unknown realm and struggling to escape, or being suspended between heaven and earth, or endlessly interrogated without reason and declared guilty without knowing the crime – these resonate far beyond Iran's borders. They echo the condition of modern humanity: seemingly free, yet caught like an insect in a web of invisible threads, constantly struggling.

And now look… in trying to explain one metaphor, I've fallen into another. And if I continue, I'll need even more metaphors to make sense of the previous ones – until I've lost track of what I was saying entirely, and all that's left is me, you, and a meaning slipping ever further away, leaving only anxiety in its place – and the inexplicable pounding of our hearts.

Fereshteh Ahmadi
Translated by Caroline Croskery

Notes

1. The demonstrations of 5th and 6th June, 1963 (aka the 15 Khordad) were protests in Iran against the arrest of Ruhollah Khomeini after his denouncement of Iranian Shah Mohammad Reza Pahlavi and Israel, which, although suppressed within days by the authorities, established the importance and power of (Shia) religious opposition to the Shah.

2. The 'Dah Shab' or Ten Nights were a series of poetry readings at the Goethe Institute in Tehran, organised by the Iranian Writers' Association which culminated in writers and some students taking to the streets, demanding an end to censorship, setting the precedent for a series of ongoing protests that culminated in the 1979 Revolution.

Oil

Nasim Marashi

Translated by Alireza Abiz

CRUDE OIL IS SHINY and sticky. Black and thick. It sticks to my body. The whiteness of my face isn't visible beneath it. It flows smoothly in the fresh warmth of early March. I glide, twist, and spin with it. Like the New Year goldfish when thousands of them are poured into a small tub. People are cheering. I dance within the oil. Nobody sees me. Crude oil is shiny and sticky. Black and thick. It sticks to my body.

The headteacher stands against the concrete wall, talking about the new directive. Opposite him is the school building, and behind it is a large oil tank. As he speaks, these thoughts come into my mind. Nasseri and I stand before him, listening. Midway through his talk, the headteacher reaches into his pockets. 'A cigarette was good for moments like these,' he says. 'Oh, exactly for times like these. Oh, what a thing the cigarette was...!' Then he sighs. For twenty years, there's been no cigarette in his pockets, yet several times a day, he reaches into his pockets out of habit. The headteacher always talks about cigarettes; whenever the situation at school gets tough, when someone says something funny, whenever an inspector is due to visit, whenever a child screams in the yard, etc... I have never smoked, but the headteacher has smoked a lot. He is 50 now and had been smoking since he was 30. Zar and Homa cigarettes. Then the oil tanks became full again, and we were sanctioned again, and no one bought our oil. Soon oil was everywhere. First in the old tanks, then in the newly built ones, then water reservoirs, city pools, park fountains, household tanks, buckets, bottles, and bowls. Sculptors built metal and glass landmarks filled with oil in squares and boulevards. They made hollow statues of the Leader and filled them with oil. They installed oil tanks on rooftops and decorated the facades of houses with oil fountains. They feared the oil would catch fire, so cigarettes, lighters, and the fireworks of Chaharshanbeh Suri[1] were all banned. That was twenty years ago. I was born that same year.

The headteacher is tall and thin. The little hair left around his head is entirely white, and the sun shines on his baldness. His nose is long, and his chin wide. He wears a wool suit and styles himself after old photos of the Leader. I've seen him in the school bathroom putting dark circles under his eyes, practising a crooked smile like the Leader's. The headteacher is our school's tourist attraction. People come from far away to watch him. He's invited to important speeches. Once, he even played the Leader in a film.

The headteacher has to reread the announcement several times from the beginning because people keep gathering around us. The headteacher is short, which is his biggest difference from the Leader. Nasseri brings him a chair. The headteacher stands on it and reads again: 'Gentlemen, I'm reading this for the last time. Please listen. Listen, gentlemen.' He claps his hands, clears his throat, and places the Leader's crooked smile on his lips. 'Honourable nation of Iran! On the hundredth anniversary of defeating the American coup, we are proud for the first time in history to return our extracted oil back to nature. This is a decisive response to Eastern, Western, Northern, and Southern countries, which haven't bought our oil for more than a hundred years. This century-long sanction is our greatest victory because instead of selling oil, we are now preserving it for the future generations, for the good children of this land…' The headteacher gestures towards the children playing in the schoolyard, maintaining the Leader's crooked smile. 'We will preserve it for the good children of this land. Therefore, tomorrow, the 19th of March, 2054, marking one hundred years since the defeat of the American coup and the glorious anniversary of the nationalisation of the oil industry, at exactly nine in the morning, the country's oil tanks in 50 desert locations will be opened and the oil will return to the earth. All compatriots are requested to attend these locations listed below, along with the oil entrusted to them and its receipts, to celebrate this innovation and national pride. In memory of our Leader, Mohammad Mosaddegh, Iran's children will forever have oil.'

People cheer. The headteacher thanks them with the Leader's crooked smile, folds the directive, and places it in his pocket. I feel myself slipping on the crude oil, black and thick, sticky and shiny, which flows quickly in this weather. I know exactly in what weather crude oil flows. In our region, it flows smoothly after the first week of March and becomes thick again by the first week of November. Oil has always existed around me, around all of us. Nasseri and I look at each other. Right now, I want to go to the wall with Nasseri and chat. Our school is the last building before the border wall. After the city ends, there is a large oil tank, a school, and two hundred metres ahead, the wall. We are under sanctions and not allowed to see beyond our borders. Nasseri and I always go near the wall and talk and try to guess what's behind it all. Maybe there are flying cars or robotic humans doing the work. Sometimes we climb atop the oil tank and watch the wall. I'm in love with the world beyond the wall. So is Nasseri. That's why I became a teacher here, to be close to the world on the other side.

When the headteacher was growing up, the wall hadn't been built yet. He always describes to us how different the land and buildings of this neighbouring country are. There's nowhere in our land where you can see this other country. Our country is surrounded entirely by a wall. In some places, like here in the desert, the wall is shorter, but where the border is mountainous, it's very tall. Sometimes we travel to see taller parts of the wall. Though we are under sanctions and can't see beyond this border, we can smell strange scents when we sit right beside it, and often guess what they might be. Sometimes, if lucky, we hear sounds from behind the wall. Nasseri and I quickly guess their origins – strange cars, perhaps. Occasionally, we see odd flying objects in the sky behind the wall – strange planes, small iron birds, flying people. When something appears in the sky, children run out of class, and we can't stop them – we don't want to stop them either. Children stand on oil barrels and scream. Nasseri and I do the same when no one is watching.

I want to go with Nasseri to the wall, but the headteacher calls us over the loudspeaker. The children scream and rush out. The day after tomorrow is the New Year, and they're excited about their holidays. Nasseri and I push through the kids. The headteacher stands by the porch edge with a list, the janitor brings out oil buckets and bottles from the basement and counts them. The headteacher reads: 'Fifty ten-litre buckets, three two-thousand-litre tanks, one hundred and twelve one-and-a-half-litre bottles...' The janitor interrupts, 'Wait, let me count, sir.'

The headteacher says, 'I dismissed the kids early to prepare the oil reserves for tomorrow. The government calculates with great precision to ensure everything is accounted for. You must also sort out your home oil. Be here tomorrow at 8am to take the kids to the celebration.'

Nasseri objects, 'But tomorrow holidays start, sir. Let the kids go with their families. I want to go with my wife.'

'Impossible,' the headteacher responds. 'What about national pride? The children must be in the front row, cheering and dressed in their special uniforms.'

'I can't accept responsibility for these kids,' I say. 'Crude oil is slippery. If they slip…'

The headteacher retorts sharply, 'Then why am I asking you to be there? It's your responsibility to prevent that.'

I like to go to the wall with Nasseri, but he rushes off home to help his wife. I walk around the oil tank, heading home. Radios broadcast the directive loudly in the streets and alleyways. The city is bustling; people are wandering about aimlessly like the New Year's fish in the tub. The city has lost its New Year's spirit. Everywhere buckets and containers are filled with oil instead of festive goods. I pass by the fish seller. He was supposed to set aside three lively goldfish for me to take home for our Haft-seen[2] table. I find his aquarium full of oil. We exchange glances, he nods; I walk on.

At home, Father stands in the middle of the hall, surrounded by containers of oil. Mother has opened an old bag and is pulling out receipts – each one proof of oil deliveries. Each receipt records the date and the amount of oil we received. It states that we keep the oil in trust for the state and in the name of the people. Once the East and West are defeated and sanctions are lifted, we should return it so the government can sell it.

My brother pulls out the oil containers hidden at the back of the closet and inside the kitchen cabinets, complaining, 'Our whole life is black. Look what they've done to people right before the New Year. If they had just sealed up those damned wells, we wouldn't have to fill our homes with oil and then dump it in the desert. Why do they even extract it when they haven't been able to sell it for a hundred years?'

Father says, 'Shut up, boy. The country's oil industry must not stop.'

Mother jumps in, panicked. 'Oh, no! I used some of the oil

from that big tanker a few times – I poured it into a tub so the baby could play in it.'

Father and my brother turn pale. My brother grabs his child, who is holding oil-filled toys in his small hands: a plastic teddy bear full of oil that inflates on one side when squeezed, and a glass ship where thick oil sloshes inside.

Father snaps, 'You're insane! Now how am I supposed to put that back?'

Mother starts crying. My brother mutters, 'If there's one thing this damned country has plenty of, it's oil. Let's go take some from the park fountain down the street.' Then he looks at me. 'You go.'

Father asks, 'What if they see him?'

My brother shrugs. 'They're dumping it all in the desert anyway. You think they care if a little is missing?'

Mother hands me a large thermos. Father warns, 'Take it quietly so no one notices.'

My brother grabs some oil and grumbles again. 'People all over the world are flying, and we're still stuck trying to store a few litres of oil in people's homes.'

Father replies, 'You're not going anywhere past the street corner. Use your legs. What do you need flying for?'

And I step out the door.

My brother is always complaining. My father is always content. My mother sometimes sides with my father, sometimes with my brother. But I – I just want to go beyond the wall.

I've always wanted to leave.

As a child, I would run down our alley and slam myself against the wall. When I got older, I would sneak up the steps of the oil tank to see a bit more of the sky beyond the wall. Now, in class, I rearrange the desks and chairs, so I face the wall while I teach. I stare at it the entire time, imagining that one day I will finally go.

Beyond the wall, the smells and sounds are different. People fly in its sky.

We are sanctioned, and no country beyond these walls allows us to enter. But I want to go. Without permission. Like my brother's wife, who left and was never heard from again.

Father says they wouldn't let her live freely beyond the wall. That they would imprison her. He says this because no one who has left has ever returned. But even if they'd imprison me, I still want to go. The only thing that stops me is my father. Ever since my brother's wife left, he has aged. One night, he came home crying, saying it was his fault for failing to keep his daughter-in-law loyal to the country. Later, I found out that they had denied him a seat at the Resistance Committee meetings. His former colleagues no longer associated with him.

Father aged suddenly. If I left, he wouldn't be able to bear another disgrace. It would kill him.

I reach the pond and the fountain. A crowd has gathered around it. Everyone stands with frightened eyes, holding containers, waiting. It's clear they've come for oil. An old man says, 'Starting tomorrow, they'll run water in the fountain again. You are all young and haven't seen it. But I remember. When there was water in the fountain, you could dip your hands in it. The water was cool. You could wash your face in it. The cats and pigeons would come to drink from it. At the end of the New Year festivities, we would release our goldfish into it.'

I walk away with my thermos, looking for a quieter fountain, and I think. And think.

I must go beyond the wall. And to make sure my family isn't disgraced, I must make everyone believe I am dead. It's the only way. I push my mind to its limits. When the headteacher was reading the directive, I saw myself slipping on the oil. That's the way. And now is the time. My corpse must slip on the oil, and I must disappear beyond the wall.

At the street corner, I find a fountain full of oil. No one is around. I fill my thermos and walk back home, thinking the whole way about my corpse. Crude oil is black and thick. Shiny and sticky. It will cling to my skin, covering my face so no one will recognise me.

I need to create a body – a corpse – and throw it into the oil. Tomorrow. I won't get another chance.

When I get home, Father has already poured oil all over the front yard. My brother and his child are asleep. Mother is ironing clothes for the celebration. She and Father are preparing their finest outfits. I open the closet. I touch my chest, then everything inside the closet. I run my hands over my arms, my legs, my face. I must build my corpse. I rummage through the closet, pulling out an ironing board, a cane, some empty bottles to stick together, a pillow to stuff its feathers into my pants. I touch my body again and whatever is in the closet. I find my belly, my fingers, the soles of my feet. But I can't find my head. I move to my clothes – shirts, pants, shoes, a hat. A large hat that will hide my eyes when I wear it. But I still don't have a head. I grab my mother's sewing box and go downstairs. By the door, I find my head. It's my nephew's ball. I touch my face. Then the ball. I pick up my head and step outside.

At dawn, I wake up beside my corpse, in the middle of the oil-covered yard. The cool morning breeze carries the oil's sharp scent, stronger than ever. The sky is still dark, and no one else is awake. I have worked through the night. Now, when the thick, sticky, shiny black oil coats my corpse, it will be identical to me. I fold it up and pack it into a large sack. I kiss my sleeping nephew. I look at Father for a long time. I take my mother's scarf and leave for school. I miss them already.

Across the street, a group of workers is cleaning up the bare land opposite the school. Others are adorning the massive oil tank with flowers. Overnight, they've installed a platform near the tank, building a space for spectators. The sound of crows fills the air. The school is empty. The janitor is still asleep. I slip into the office to hide my corpse. A strange smell lingers in the air. Suddenly, I see the headteacher sitting inside. He has placed a mirror in front of him and is practising the Leader's crooked smile. His hair is neatly trimmed, and he's wearing a brand-new cashmere suit. Dark circles shadow his eyes. When I greet him, I notice a faint orange light flickering between his fingers. The headteacher is startled. He starts to say something, but I pretend I haven't seen anything. I clutch my corpse tightly and leave the office. I walk to the wall. How beautiful that our morning and the morning beyond the wall are the same. That our sky is shared.

I hold my corpse close, lean against the wall, and listen. I imagine that when I finally reach the other side, if they don't imprison me, I will travel through all the borderless countries of the world. I will travel so far that one day, I will return and find myself at this very wall again. I imagine that whenever I miss home, I will come back and press myself against the wall. And then I will call out to Nasseri, who will have come here alone, thinking of me. Nasseri will hear me from the other side of the wall. We will talk. I will ask about my parents. And I will tell him everything that lies beyond the wall. Even after I leave, I will return to this wall and weave dreams. Dreams of the world on this side of the wall.

Little by little, the schoolyard fills up. Children in their uniforms arrive, followed by parents carrying oil containers. Government cars pull up. Workers. Policemen. Near the massive oil tank, they are setting up the speaker's platform. Several trucks arrive, each carrying smaller tanks. Then Nasseri appears, hand-in-hand with his wife. He scans the crowd until he spots me. He walks to the wall and calls my name. It is nearly 9am. The children are waiting for us.

The school is crowded. The headteacher and the janitor sit

in the back of a truck that is hauling the school's oil reserves towards the platform. I clutch my corpse and line up the children. I check their shoes to make sure they won't slip. I worry they might fall, that the thick, black oil will coat their bodies. I am unsure of their safety. I find a rope and tie their arms together. We walk towards the platform. The whole city has gathered with their oil containers. My father. My mother. The New Year's fish seller. The old man from the fountain. My brother, holding his son, stands a little further away. Nasseri and his wife stand at the front of the cheering crowd, twenty students dressed in matching uniforms behind them. A few policemen weave through the crowd, checking receipts and verifying the oil containers. I hold my suitcase tightly, pulling the children behind me. I don't trust the rope. I tell them not to let go of each other's hands. I walk to Nasseri. I take the hand of the first child in my line and place it in the hand of the last child in his. 'Take care of each other,' I tell them. Then I step away with my corpse. The headteacher stands on the platform, next to the mayor. A recording of a speech from a hundred years ago – an old speech of the Leader – plays over the loudspeakers. The crowd cheers. The headteacher nods in time with the voice, as if it were his own. Occasionally, he mouths the words. Then the Prime Minister's voice comes on, announcing the start of the celebration across the country. He reads the directive for the 'liberation' of oil. I weave my way through the crowd with my corpse. I pass Nasseri and his wife. I pass the headteacher and the mayor. I pass my father and mother. I pass the New Year's fish seller.

I reach the massive oil tank. I stand just beneath the pump pipe. I remove the corpse from my bag and hold it in my arms. The Prime Minister finishes his speech.

The mayor hands the headteacher a small bottle of oil – to be ceremonially poured onto the desert in the Leader's memory. The headteacher smiles his crooked smile and tips the bottle.

The crowd erupts in cheers. I watch them. I watch my students waving little flags. I watch my father, his face beaming with pride. I commit that expression to memory. I see my mother, as always, searching the crowd for my brother's child. My chest tightens.

The mayor raises his hand. 'Everyone, prepare yourselves for the sound of the cannon,' he announces. At the cannon's signal, the massive tank will begin to empty. Then the smaller tanks will be drained. Then the people will gift their stored oil onto the desert in the name of independence. I lift my corpse from the bag. I whisper to myself: Crude oil is black and thick.

Shiny and sticky. It will cling to my corpse. The people hold their breath. I press the corpse to my chest. I lean against the tank. I look around. No one is paying attention to me.

The cannon fires.

A deafening roar echoes as the giant pumps activate, sucking the oil from the tank. A flood of crude oil spills onto the ground. Black and thick. Shiny and sticky. The air is thick with the suffocating stench of sulphur. The people's cheers are drowned in the roar of the cascading oil. I hold tightly to my corpse. The oil spreads quickly, carving black channels through the desert. I reach out. The current grabs my corpse. It begins to slip from my grasp. I tighten my grip. I think of the world beyond the wall. My head spins. The oil carries my corpse away. Crude oil is slippery. I watch my corpse as I lose my balance. I slip and fall into the oil.

My corpse and I spin together in the thick, black, sticky oil. We crash into each other and separate. Like the New Year's fish when thousands of them are thrown into a tiny tub. We swirl in the oil. The people's cheers rise and fall. Crude oil is black and thick. Shiny and sticky. It clings to our bodies.

I don't know how long I drift in the oil before the flow stops. I collapse, motionless, on the ground. Hands grab at my blackened, sticky body. They lift me up. They pass me from one set of hands to another. Through the noise, I hear my brother's child calling out. I hear my mother crying. I hear Nasseri. A warm hand grasps mine. Then lets go. The headteacher's voice rings out: 'People! Our independence has always been won with martyrs. For a hundred years, our young have sacrificed themselves for freedom. This is the first martyr of our great oil liberation.' I want to open my eyes. I can't. I think of the world beyond the wall. I have lost my chance. Tears fill my eyes. The thick, shiny oil clings to my face. No one can see me crying. I pray that no one finds my corpse. The headteacher is still speaking. Martyr. Martyr. My mother must be terrified. I struggle to lift my arm. The crowd erupts in cheers.

The headteacher's speech is lost in their voices. They lift me higher. They place me on the platform. They hold me upright. In the front row, the children are shouting: 'The Oil Statue.'

Notes

1. Chaharshanbeh Suri is a traditional Iranian festival celebrated on the eve of the last Wednesday before the Persian New Year. It involves people jumping over a bonfire.

2. **Haft-seen** is a traditional Persian arrangement of seven symbolic items, each starting with the Persian letter 'S', displayed on a table during the celebration of Nowruz, the Persian New Year. These items represent various values, such as health, prosperity, and renewal, and are meant to bring good fortune for the coming year.

Eye for an Eye

Sholeh Wolpé

TODAY, WE RUN.

MAMAN has packed our life into three small bundles, each wrapped in thermal cloth that disguises weight and temperature, just in case we're scanned. Baba pulls on a pair of mandatory tight blue jeans and tucks in a T-shirt a size too small for his belly.

'See what they've reduced us to?'

He says this with disgust to no one in particular, but I sense it's aimed at me – as if I, too, bear some blame for what has happened to Iran.

Maman folds her chador into tiny squares until it could be anything: a folded scarf, a blouse, a dress.

'What about Golnaz?' I ask.

Maman widens her tired green eyes, throws up her eyebrows and flicks her gaze to Baba. I guess my sister isn't coming. Not even to say goodbye.

'She's the dirt under my nails,' says Baba. 'Didn't I tell you never to mention her name? Not even after I'm dead.' He picks up the bundle Maman has handed him and angrily motions us towards the door.

Two hours past midnight is the darkest hour of the night. Maybe this night is going to last the rest of my life. I take a last look at my room, all the things I'm being forced to leave behind. My books, vintage CDs, charcoal drawings, the heart-shaped pillow my best friend gave me on my tenth birthday, and that magazine, forbidden by Baba, hidden under my mattress.

We step into the night. The street outside is under curfew – enforced by neighbourhood drones, though none are overhead at this moment. The only sounds are the wind and the soft bark of distant dogs. The digital lampposts have flickered to economy mode, so their sensors fail to identify our ID signatures. Everyone is in bed, floating in dreams. Unlike us. Tomorrow, they will wake up in their own beds, sheets smelling of home. They will sit at their kitchen tables and eat fresh bread from the bakery up the alley and feta cheese with quince jam.

We climb into an old blue Mercedes, retrofit with a silent engine. It smells like cooked rice. The dash reads 2:05am, 25/6/2052. The driver, a woman in a sleeveless pink blouse, pulls her bleached curls into a bun and fastens them with a heat-sensitive pin. She turns with sharp energy and looks at Baba.

'We have your money,' says Baba.

'Let your wife hold it,' the woman replies. 'She'll pay me when we get there.'

Baba nods and fastens his seatbelt. The woman turns around and stares ahead. She doesn't start the engine. She just sits there, waiting. Baba takes a deep breath, pulls the packet of money out of his pocket, and shoves it into Maman's hands.

'There,' he says to the woman. 'Satisfied?'

'Now go shave,' she says. 'The border drones read stubble as resistance markers. You don't want to get flagged.'

Baba runs a hand over his cheeks and chin. 'It grows too fast.'

She shrugs. 'So carry a portable shaver next time. The government gives them out for a reason.'

No one talked to Baba like this in the old days. But the old days are archived now – offline, unreachable.

★

Back in 2049, when I was nine and confounded by what was happening in Iran, people Baba called 'extremists' were gaining ground. Young, determined, and fearless, they sabotaged mosque networks, cracked secure clouds, and turned the holy city of Qom into something unrecognisable – a city of shadows and ash.

The last time I saw my sister Golnaz was just before the uprising. She was a university student then and had secretly joined the underground movement rumoured to be backed by the Saudi Feminine Front.

That day, after Maman had cleared the lunch table, Golnaz didn't dash off as usual. She lingered, poured Baba a cup of tea and watched him tap quietly on his scroll-pad.

'Sentencing some poor girl again?' she asked. 'Tap. Bang. Off she goes.'

'Don't you need to be somewhere?' he said, not really asking.

'You don't even see what's coming, do you?' she asked. 'Well, when it arrives, there'll be no mercy. Not for the mullahs like you. Not for the Basij.[1] There will be unflinching justice. An eye for an eye, a tooth for a tooth.'

'So now you're quoting the Torah? Are you a Jew these days?' Baba snorted, adjusting his clergy cape around his belly.

'That's Hammurabi's code. Law of retaliation where punishment matches the crime.'

'Crime? We have democracy, fair elections. People choose their leader, follow their faith.'

He popped a whole date in his mouth and chewed slowly.

'Fair elections? Democracy?' Golnaz repeated, laughing dryly. She took off her gold-rimmed glasses, wiped the lenses with the edge of her uniform, a faded brown tunic with smart-thread identifiers at the cuffs.

'Aren't those words a bit too big for your mouth, Mullah

Dolati? You who sent people to rot in draconian cells? Do you really think what dangles between your legs qualifies you to speak for God?'

I took off my game headset and stared. She had never spoken to him like this.

Baba shook his head. 'This big revolution of yours has given you a filthy mouth. Have you no shame? Disrespecting your father, country, and God?'

Golnaz let out a laugh. Not the kind real people make. The kind screen characters force when they want you to know they are about to pull the trigger.

'There is no country, Baba,' she said. 'No God either. Just us. And now, we're the ones writing the codes. Your version was evil.'

She stepped forward. 'Lashes, prison, fear, rape, executions–'

'Which did you experience, exactly?' Baba interrupted. 'In your privileged little life?'

Outside, a voice-activated delivery drone buzzed low over the alley. Someone shouted up to it in frustration.

Golnaz went to the window, opened the shades and looked out. 'There's no difference between me and them,' she said. 'We are one now. A single, brutal machine.'

'Ungrateful little shit,' Baba growled. 'You were protected. Fed. Educated.'

'And gaslit.' She unbuttoned her uniform, pulled it off, and threw it at Baba's feet. Underneath she wore red gym shorts and a sleeveless white shirt.

'It's a hundred degrees out,' she said. 'You get to dress like that, but we? We have to cover up or else we get scanned, fined, and tracked.'

She stepped close enough to make him flinch. 'We sweat and piss our pants from fear. But it's all going to be over soon. We'll give you a taste of your own shit-medicine.'

For a moment, I thought he would hit her, but instead he came over to me and put his hand on my shoulder.

'Look at your sister,' he said to me. 'All that hatred. That's what happens when you abandon Islam.'

'Abandon?' Golnaz laughed. 'Hell, no! We'll rewrite it. Just like you did. For centuries.'

She then looked at me and said, 'I'm leaving this shithole. Come with me, I'll take care of you.'

Baba stepped in front of me and shoved her back. She lost her balance and fell. Her head hit the edge of the glass coffee table and blood started to stream from her temple. Maman rushed in, saw the blood, and let out a cry so sharp it activated the kitchen's assistance bot, which chirped once and shut off again.

'What am I going to do with this family?' she wailed, pounding her fists against her own forehead.

Golnaz picked up her uniform and wiped her face with it. 'Maman,' she said, voice trembling, 'escape while you still can. Join us.'

'Join? Join who?' asked Maman. 'A bunch of schoolgirls running around dressed like carnival whores? Don't you get it? The drones will have your face and they'll come for you. Nowhere will be safe. If you don't care about your own life, then at least think of your father's abroo.'

Golnaz used to get furious with our mother when she talked like that. She would come to my room, crying: 'We are prisoners of abroo.'

That was a word I didn't quite get when I was younger: water over the face, on the face, protecting the face. But she explained it to me over and over until I did. What I had thought meant 'face' was really a word for 'façade', the outer presentation. Regardless of any chaos, dirt or wrongdoings within a family, the façade or the face to present to the world must be impeccable. Shame is an indelible stain that could tarnish a family's abroo forever.

But that day, Golnaz didn't get angry, she didn't cry. She simply stared at Maman with a peculiar expression on her face, as if she was from another planet, another life, another reality.

'Come with me,' she said again. Her voice was tender, pleading. 'We can help you. We've learned how to deprogram. Undo centuries of garbage fed to us like hay to donkeys. Don't you see, Maman? We've done it! We've organised, we've armed ourselves with a new weapon and we're winning.'

Golnaz held her forefinger and thumb an inch apart and brought them close to Maman's eyes.

'We're this close.'

Maman looked at my sister's delicate fingers for a long moment, perhaps considering the possibility of what she was saying. Then, as if suddenly stirred from a dream, she slapped Golnaz. Blood from her daughter's temple streaked across her hand. Maman recoiled in shock – as though realising it was her own, too. Anger drained from her face, and she collapsed onto the floor and began to wail.

'Get out of my house,' said Baba, his voice hoarse with wrath.

Golnaz's face emptied. The absence of any human expression in a moment like that was telling of what was to come. She turned to me again and said, 'Come with me… before it's too late.'

I wanted to ask, 'Too late for what?' But my tongue wouldn't move. I wanted to choose them both, to go with my sister into that promising unknown, but also to stay, right there, where it felt safe and familiar. Baba pulled me behind him, and I let him.

★

My father gets back into the car, clean-shaven and smelling of olive soap. The woman glances at him, nods, and taps the ignition. The engine hums to life – soundless and cold. Tehran's streetlights flicker on predictive cycles. Biometric patrols drift down wide avenues accompanied by female soldiers. I stare out the window, hoping to catch sight of my sister.

Shops are shuttered, but still alive with neon signs: *Mahnaz*

Cakes - Voted #1 in New Iran; Abadi Kebab – Why Cook At Home?; Ladan Drycleaning – Clean, Fresh, Easy; Melody Electronics – We Fix It All. I'm overwhelmed with a strange sense of nostalgia for what we haven't yet fully left. Is it too late for me to jump out and run? Abandon Baba? Baba, who protected me? Baba, who sent girls like me to re-education pods, and worse?

★

'In the old days, they raped young women before executing them – because killing a virgin was haram.' I read that in a magazine a woman stuffed into my backpack on Liberty Square.

This was a year after the 2051 revolution. She wore a *Woman, Life, Freedom* band around her arm, her headband shimmering with the colours of the uprising.

'Join the New Iran,' she said. 'You haven't crossed over yet – I can see that.'

I was eleven. In baggy clothes and still hiding behind Baba's codes and firewalls.

Golnaz hadn't come back for me. Maybe she was dead. Maybe she didn't want to have anything to do with me – with us – anymore. I hadn't left with her that day, and perhaps that made me a traitor in her eyes. A spy in the making. A brainwashed piece of shit. Maybe I was all of those things. Maybe. But nothing is ever that simple.

'The struggle is over!' the woman had shouted at my back. 'Freedom is yours to claim!'

I remember locking myself in my room that day, taking out the magazine. The cover showed Iran's women's national soccer team, arms linked, sweat shining on their foreheads as they held up the 2052 World Cup trophy. Under the Islamic Republic, they couldn't even attend a match. Now, it said, men could attend – but only if accompanied by a woman.

I read the whole issue – twice, then three more times. Articles on women-led startups, biometric safety wear, poetry channels. A feature on Shahrnush Parsipur, whose banned books and prison memoir were now taught in public schools. She'd survived Evin and other prisons. She'd written through years of poverty in exile. But hard as they tried, they couldn't delete her.

Baba once said, 'We only want to bring Islam to men and women, equally.'

He also said lying was a sin.

When I asked him why people hated clerics, he said, 'Sometimes people are like naughty children. A little punishment sets them back on the right path. It's for their own good, but they don't see that. So, they get mad.'

And I believed him.

After the revolution, Baba changed all the passwords. He locked the media node and installed outdated firmware. He unplugged us from the grid and surrounded us only with those who still called him *Mullah Dolati*.

The men who used to guard the state were gone – rehabilitated, vanished, exiled on rubber rafts with no GPS tags. Many of Baba's friends, once feared clerics, were sent to the same prisons they'd once filled. Only this time, the guards were women. They called it *therapy*.

Golnaz's words haunted me. 'Eye for an eye, tooth for a tooth.'

But the opposite of injustice isn't more injustice.

Why couldn't anyone see that?

★

One week before our escape, while preparing the evening meal, I asked Maman, 'Is Baba a good man?'

'He is. You can be a good person but still do bad things.'

'I'm glad I don't have to wear the chador[2] anymore,' I said. 'Does that make me bad?' I hoped she'd say no, but instead she took a handful of rice and dumped it into the soup.

'Chastity and purity are a woman's privilege, not burden,' she said. 'Our bodies aren't the same as men's. We emanate rays that drive men crazy. So the Prophet made a law to protect us. He said, "Hide your allure." That way, you're safe and don't make trouble for men. And when you finally get married, your powers will be doubly strong. You can use them on your husband to get what you want.'

'Do you get what you want?'

I asked this because I knew she didn't.

'I do.'

It was such an obvious lie it made the air leave the kitchen.

I nodded and turned back to the onions. My eyes burned, and I let the tears come. Maman wiped them away and gently pushed me aside.

'Let me. I don't mind the tears.' She wanted an excuse to cry.

I stepped back and thought about her sister – the one who married a Baha'i and converted to his religion. They said she was a Zionist spy. It was an outrageous accusation and Baba knew it. But he didn't stop them from putting the noose around her neck. He saw the conversion of his sister-in-law to a heretic faith as a stain on his family honour. He took his abroo that seriously.

As Maman's tears fell onto the onions, I felt my stomach twist. I turned away and vomited on the floor.

★

Now in the car, we speed towards the city's edge. The plan is to reach Khoy by nightfall, then Maku, and from there – on foot through the mountains to Turkey. Baba says Turkey still holds onto the Holy Faith. But I heard him tell Maman, 'It's spreading. We may have to go further. West. Some place where women are still sane.'

The driver goes too fast.

'Slow down, sister,' Baba says. 'You don't want to get pulled over.'

'Don't call me that,' she barks. 'I'm not your sister.' She doesn't slow down.

Baba is in a bad mood. Maybe he is scared. He pulls on his crotch, curses his tight pants, and adjusts himself on the seat. Past Abadi Street, the freeway lurks ahead, but instead of going straight towards it, the driver swerves and makes a sharp right into an alley. A pair of high-beam lights floods the windscreen.

'What the hell?' Baba unbuckles, ready to flee.

Too late. Our car screeches to a stop before an armoured SUV. Guards step out, guns drawn.

'End of the line,' the driver says.

She turns around and looks at Baba. 'You don't remember me, do you? Of course not. I was just one of thousands. Time to taste your own medicine, Mullah Dolati.'

Guards open the car doors on both sides. Maman and I are pulled from the car. She says nothing – too scared, or maybe too relieved.

Baba is dragged from the other side. He looks at us as if we betrayed him. As if we brought this ruin.

The guards – women – don't speak to him. They shove him into the SUV and shut the door. No goodbye.

The tallest of the guards, with braided hair like Frida Kahlo's, takes Maman's left hand, slips off her wedding ring and flicks it into the gutter.

'You're free, sister,' she says. 'Take your daughter and go home.'

Notes

1. A paramilitary volunteer militia within Iran's Islamic Revolutionary Guard Corps (IRGC) sphere and one of its five branches.
2. A long, loose outer garment worn by women.

For Maliheh

Behnam Yousefpour

Translated by poupeh missaghi

NOW YOU CAN GO lose yourself. Dr Mosaddegh is waiting for
you in the Blazer truck. Your memory of me has turned into
a set of eyes, eyes watching over you from above as you go
down the stairs, your hand sliding on the railing that swirls like
a snail shell. You turn, along with your shadow, knowing that
the light from the chandelier will keep with you all the way to
the bottom. You put a hand in your pocket and, before getting
all the way down, still turning your feet on the stairs, you feel
the coldness of the knife's metal and its horn handle. You shut
your eyes at the blade's thirst for unspilled blood, and you
forgive yourself. Not giving a damn about the trace of blood
on your eyebrow, not wiping away the veil of tears from your
eyes, not counting the stairs – the way you always do, either
going up or down – you imagine inserting the car key into the
ignition, then move forward in time to the turning on of the
engine of the truck. The sound of the eight-cylinder engine
swirls around your head and with a light step on the gas pedal,
you reach the gate at the end of the path. In the diamond-
shaped glass of the front door, turned into a mirror in the
darkness of the night, you see yourself. You pull up your
overcoat zipper. You pull down the woollen black hat on your

hair, still full but now completely white. You smile at the old man in the mirror and finally clean the tears from your eyes. You look away from yourself, open the door, and walk outside. I leap down from my position up above you and, through the half-open door not yet shut by the last push of its hinge, I too burst out.

★

When the truck stops, a cloud of dust rises, and joining the already dusty air, it becomes a canopy over the young man selling gas, soda, and cigarettes in his kiosk at the three-way intersection. He has a mask on. He looks up for a second before looking down again at his mobile phone. The driver takes three pills from a canister and swallows them all at once.

'Mosaddegh's Ahmad Abad!'[1]

Clearly at a critical stage of his game, the young man raises his hand to signal the driver to wait. Then a frown appears on his face, and he throws his phone onto the counter.

'I lost! What do you want, Haji?'[2]

'Don't you dare call me Haji! I asked for the way to Mosaddegh's Ahmad Abad!'

The young man steps closer and leans on the passenger side window.

'Just Ahmad Abad! There is no Mosaddegh there anymore, there are no humans there!'

The old man looks in the mirror. He notices the deserted Abik Cement Factory. In his head, a woman's voice says, *Morteza! It was right here, right around this very factory!*

Morteza turns around and looks at the other side of the road. The dust has turned the air brown.

'Want me to fill it up?'

Morteza looks at the young man.

'Take your mask off and let me see you! You said there was no one there?! What's your name?'

The young man pulls the mask down.

'Where there's no water, there's no humans. Everything has dried up there. I'm Ahmad. What's your name, dear old man?'

Morteza laughs.

'Don't be fooled by my white hair. Let's arm wrestle. I'll use one hand, you both.'

Ahmad laughs a winner's laugh.

'You totally look seventy. Come on. Let's do it.'

The young man brings his hand in through the window. The two men's fingers get tangled into one another's.

'I said you should use both hands, Ahmad Agha!'

Ahmad keeps smiling and does the countdown. The old man and the young man put all their power into their fingers. A frown shapes between Ahmad's eyebrows. His face turns red. Morteza slowly bends Ahmad's hand outward. Beginning to lose, Ahmad raises his second hand halfway to support his first but changes his mind. He laughs and lets go of the game.

'I was fooled by your white hair. A cold Pepsi on me.'

A few military cars pass them by in a file. Ahmad spits on the ground. 'Fuck them all!'

Morteza looks away from the train of cars. 'Where are they off to?'

Ahmad drags his feet over his spit and spreads its wetness all over the ground. 'You look surprised! Have you been abroad or something?' He looks up from the trace of his spit, and his eyes meet Morteza's.

'I was serving time. I went in with black hair and came out white.'

He runs his hand over his hair. Ahmad keeps staring.

'May they all be cursed!' Ahmad says. 'When the Supreme Leader finally kicked the bucket, the country fell into the hands of these bastards. They uprooted everything, dried everything out. Now they sit in their air-conditioned air-filtered cars, without feeling the heat or the dust, and keep parading in front of us.'

He takes a deep breath.

'Look! Take this side road until you get to a fork. Take the left one all the way to the end. You'll arrive at a mosque. It used to have an automated muezzin which, before the electricity shutdowns, used to do the call to prayer three times a day for an emptied-out village!'

He runs towards the kiosk and comes back with a Pepsi.

'For my loss!'

Morteza takes the bottle. Ahmad holds his gaze on Morteza's hand.

'You didn't say as much, but I know exactly where you're headed. After the mosque, go right. The garden is right there. The villagers have held it in respect. It hasn't been ransacked, though not much was left to begin with.'

Morteza takes a gulp of the Pepsi. 'You don't have much physical strength,' he says, 'but you've got a good brain. I might not see you again, but I won't forget you, Ahmad.'

Ahmad takes a step back and pulls his mask back up. The truck starts up. Morteza watches Ahmad in the rearview mirror as he gets lost in the rising dust.

It is autumn. Like it was 30 years ago, when the trees still had leaves, and the leaves had turned yellow and had begun to fall in Kakh Street and the others around it. We would leave our house at the end of the side street, and the leaves would rustle under our feet. When we reached the main street, you would turn your head to the left and greet the house that had replaced Dr Mosaddegh's house, not willing to swap this one-sided kinship with the absent leader for anything else. You could still hear the sounds of history in that street. From the very first bullets of the coup d'état shot at 5pm on the 28th of Mordad, 1332[3] to the thugs and prostitutes joining the military to take over Kakh Street, to the military truck hitting the gate of house No. 109, to Prime Minister Mosaddegh and his cabinet members escaping through the rooftop – you remembered it all. Whatever there was to read and listen to and watch about that day, you knew them all, they all manifested in front of your eyes. And it would make you feel a lump in your throat and you would turn your rage into a drag of your cigarette, and would promise me, Maliheh, that you would eventually exhume Dr Mosaddegh's body, temporarily buried, as if on loan, in his Ahmad Abad estate, and, per his wishes, take it to Ebn-e Babviyeh Cemetery to be buried next to the dead of the 13th of Tir, 1331,[4] the men who had been killed in Baharestan Square because of their loyalty to Dr Mosaddegh. And now it is autumn again. For the past 30 years in prison, you kept this dream alive in your head. Alongside that other dream which was tied to me and smelled of blood. You did not lose momentum. Every day you exercised hard and the whiter your hair got, the more you tried to stop old age from conquering your body.

You arrive at the village. You pass by the mosque. A mangy dog curled upon itself is busy eating its own shit for lack of any other food. Listlessly, it raises his head, its eyes meeting yours for a moment. The wind picks up, raising more dust in the air. You reach into the glove compartment, bring out a lông fabric,[5] and wrap it around your face. As you pull it down a bit to uncover your eyes, you notice the green gate to Dr Mosaddegh's garden. You stop. The dog holds its gaze on you from afar. You get out of the car. As soon as you stand tall, the damned dizziness and all the voices from the past come rushing back to you. The ones that have accompanied you all these years since the nightmarish evening of the attack and the elbow blow, that you have failed to get rid of, even by hitting your head on the walls of the solitary confinement. You take out three more pills and swallow them down with the remainder of the Pepsi. A lock is hanging from the gate. You bring out a crowbar from the truck, put it under the lock, and break it open with one move. You push, and both doors of the gate are thrown wide open. Now you stand at the top of the gravelled pathway that winds through the dried trees of the garden all the way to the mansion. From somewhere outside the village, my rasping screeches reach your ears, calling for you, 'Morteza!' You turn your head towards my voice. Then silence takes over, and with it the illusions brought up by the pills. You run towards the truck.

He starts off towards the mansion. The dizziness of the pills rushes to his eyes. He double-sees every tree, drives through the doubled dried-up garden, then brakes in front of the mansion. He pulls out the shovel and pickaxe from the back of the truck where he had hidden them under a tarpaulin, then walks up the stairs. Cupping his hands, he looks inside through the windows. It is empty inside. He kicks the door open and enters. It is cold in there. Silent. With the high ceilings, his footsteps reverberate in the space. He knows the way to the room that was used to welcome guests. He opens the wooden door, and Dr Mosaddegh's tomb is right there in the middle, with a picture of him and a flag of Iran on the wall. He says, 'Hello.' Someone responds to him. It is the voice of Dr Mosaddegh, using the same tone he once used to address fellow members of parliament, speaking of establishing an independent government, asking for the revival of a constitutional system, one in which the king did not meddle in the country's affairs. When Dr Mosaddegh's 'hello' fades in the air, Morteza takes off his coat and hangs it on the back of a chair. He picks up the pickaxe and immediately makes his first strike on the tombstone. The sound of the pickaxe echoes around the room, hits the walls, and comes back. He strikes harder a second and third time. Each sound finds its way around the room, joining others and weaving a thread above his head. He removes the broken pieces of the stone and begins to shatter the concrete that covers the soil underneath. First with the shovel and then with his hands, he pulls the pieces out. He keeps going, not noticing the scars on his palms. When he moves the last bit of concrete, the wooden corner of the casket reveals itself. He grabs the corroded wood, pulls it all the way, and breaks it. The casket shakes, causing the skull inside to roll around until it faces Morteza. The empty eye socket of the skull stares at him. He closes his eyes, removes the lông mask and dries off the sweat on his face and the back of his neck. He cleans the blood from his hands with the fabric. He sweeps his hair off his face with his fingers. The remaining blood on his hand leaves a crimson trace on the white of his hair. He opens his eyes slowly. There is no trace of the skull in the casket anymore. Instead, there is Dr Mosaddegh himself, his skull covered with flesh and skin, his eyes closed. Morteza panics and, still kneeling, retreats from the tomb.

'Dear Doctor! Mr. Mosaddegh! Can you hear me?'

Dr Mosaddegh's eyelids twitch and open slowly. Morteza dares to get closer. His eyes meet the doctor's eyes, who squints and stares at Morteza.

'Who are you, sir?'

'I'm Morteza!'

'Morteza? Which Morteza? Where are the others?'

Morteza continues removing more pieces of the wood from the casket. 'There are no others, Doctor,' he says. 'It's just you and me.'

He takes Dr Mosaddegh's hand and helps him to sit up.

'I don't know what it is I'm seeing right now! But you, my dear Doctor, you have been dead for 87 years, and I'm here to take your will to heart and move your body, I mean you, to Ebn-e Babviyeh Cemetery.'

Mosaddegh looks at the shroud around his body.

'What is this?!' he demands. 'Sir, I should have proper clothes on the second floor of the house.'

Morteza gets up and runs towards the stairs.

'A suit and, of course, a walking stick. You should be able to find them.'

His body in pain, Mosaddegh gets out of the casket.

Wrapping the half-rotten shroud around him, he stands in front of his picture.

'Is the boy still alive?'

Morteza comes downstairs with the clothes and the walking stick.

'Which boy?'

'Mohammad Reza, the King!'

Morteza sneers.

'No, my dear Doctor. He too has been dead, for seventy-three years.'

Dr Mosaddegh looks around the room.

'Bastard! Who has succeeded him then? Tell me, are the Pahlavis ruling now or have the Qajars taken back the reign?'

Morteza reaches Dr Mosaddegh.

'Neither the Pahlavis, nor the Qajars! In 1357,[6] the Islamic Revolution took place. Now, the mullahs rule the country.'

Morteza helps Mosaddegh into his trousers. Mosaddegh holds on to his shoulders.

'Look, old man! As you yourself said, I'm much older than you, so you should show some respect and not joke around with me.'

Morteza keeps helping him with the trousers. 'What joking, Doctor? I'm an old man who was released from the prison today after thirty years and I've come directly here to see you.'

A frown forms between Mosaddegh's eyebrows.

'The mullahs in the government?! So, Kashani[7] finally got what he wanted.'

Morteza throws Mosaddegh's cloak over his shoulder. 'Right now, we are under military rule.'

'You mean a coup d'état and the rule of the army?'

'Which army?! Sepah, the Islamic Sepah forces!'

Mosaddegh remains silent. Morteza gives him his walking stick, and, holding on to it, Mosaddegh begins to walk around the room towards his own grave.

'So, there's a state of siege. What do you do for a living?'

Morteza grabs his coat from the back of the chair.

'Maliheh, my wife, and I were both journalists, members of the National Party. In 1401, on the twenty-fifth of Shahrivar,[8] a young woman, named Mahsa, was arrested by the morality police; they accused her of wearing her hijab improperly. She died after being hit by them in the head. An uprising started all around the country and people came to the streets. The regime, like during your time, brought out all its thugs. They hit, killed, and imprisoned people. We were just doing our job. But they opposed journalism to the core. Exactly like the day of the coup in 1332 when they invaded newspaper offices. They attacked our house in the middle of the night, breaking things, hitting us, and taking us both into custody. First, they sentenced me to execution, but then the verdict was changed to thirty years in prison. It ended this morning, and that was that.'

Outside, the sun is setting. Mosaddegh's eyes have filled with tears.

'Eternal Misery!' he sighs. 'The filthy moles who have their eyes set on money and promises of a free ride! Add religion to the mix, and you have a disaster on your hands. I saw that in Kashani's eyes. I heard the mullah went to my house the day after the coup to take photographs with General Zahedi.'[9]

Morteza steps closer to Dr Mosaddegh.

'It wasn't just photographs. There's also a video remaining from that day.'[10]

Mosaddegh leans on his walking stick.

'What happened to your wife? Where is she now? You said she was called Maliheh?'

When Maliheh's name is uttered, a scream swirls inside Morteza's head. He covers his ears with his hands and squats down. Frightened, Mosaddegh holds Morteza's shoulders.

'Are you okay, my dear man?! What's going on?'

Morteza raises his hand to show it was nothing serious.

Mosaddegh looks away towards the sunset.

'Look at us! Two old men finding each other in this sunset, coming to each other's rescue!'

He grabs Morteza under his arms and helps him get up. 'You are the boss now, old man. Tell me what we should do.'

Morteza laughs. His laughter turns into a lump in his throat. He embraces Mosaddegh. In the half-lit part of the room, the two old men allow their tears to flow. The trembling of their shoulders could have been seen from a distance.

Morteza covers the casket he has placed in the back of the truck with the tarpaulin. Mosaddegh looks around at the withered garden overtaken by the sound of the crows. Morteza opens the passenger door and cleans the dust off the leather seat with the lông fabric. Mosaddegh gets in. Morteza sits at the wheel. He pulls out a CD from the glove compartment and puts it in the stereo. Mosaddegh looks at the CD in bewilderment.

'It is the same thing as the gramophone records of your time. Just a bit smaller. What would you like to listen to?'

Mosaddegh pauses, then turns towards Morteza.

'Qamar![11] Let's listen to a nice Qamar song!'

When the song reaches its tasnif[12] part, Morteza looks at Mosaddegh who has leaned his head on the walking stick and is whispering under his breath, 'Oh you the dawn nightingale, start your cry / refresh the wound in my heart.'

Morteza turns on the truck's lights. They start moving down the drive. The garden, and the mansion in its midst, sink into the darkness of the night.

★

I arrive at our house and put the key in the lock. The gate doesn't open. I push it with all my force and finally manage to open it. Thirty years of rained-on soil has piled behind the gate. I look at the garden. The small flowerbed is full of weeds,

32

and the lonely persimmon tree has dried up. The Blazer truck is still there under the parking shade. I walk towards the building, take the two steps up from the garden, walk across the terrace, and turn the doorknob. It is open. I walk inside. Time has frozen here. I switch on the light. It doesn't come on. A DVD cover is lying in front of the TV screen. We had been watching Costa-Gavras's *State of Siege*. I pick up the cover and look at Yves Montand's picture. The film's soundtrack begins to play in my head. I remember the scene in which the interrogator says, 'You claim to defend freedom and democracy, but your methods — war, fascism, and torture. Do you agree, Mr Santore?' I whistle the song under my breath and look at the ruins of what was once upon a time our home. Overturned wardrobes, toppled sofas, pulled-out drawers, scattered books. I walk to the bedroom. Maliheh's nightgown is on the bed. My knees begin to tremble. I sit at the edge of the bed. I hold Maliheh's nightgown in my hands. I bury my head in it and breathe it in. That's it. 'It' is Maliheh's scent. I bring the gown down. It is wet with my tears. A small photo frame is upside-down on the bedside table. I pick it up. It holds a picture of Maliheh and me. I have embraced her with one arm and pulled her towards myself, and we are laughing. I go to the desk drawer. It's right there. The switchblade with the horn handle that we had bought on our trip to Zanjan. When Maliheh asked me what use I would have for a knife after a lifetime of being a journalist, I said it was just for peace of mind. Maybe one day we might have to become despots and change course, and we both laughed. I wrap the knife in the nightgown and put them by the photo frame. I find the truck keys. I knew the battery would be dead, so on my way home, I borrowed a battery to jumpstart the truck from Akbar, who still owns the battery shop down the street, and who burst into tears seeing me and my whitened hair. I draw out some sludgy water from the small pond and pour it over the truck windscreen. A dead goldfish slides down the glass. I attach the cables to the batteries. I turn the ignition. It doesn't work. A second time. Third… Finally, it starts up. I step on the gas pedal. The roar of the eight-cylinder engine echoes through the front yard. I need to get out of here.

★

It is nighttime. They reach a checkpoint. Morteza asks Mosaddegh to pretend to have passed out. A soldier orders them to stop. He asks for identification. Morteza looks into the soldier's eyes.

'My father is not feeling well. I left the house in a rush. I forgot to bring my documents.'

The soldier looks at Morteza.

'Aren't you too old for your father to be alive?!'

He lowers his head and looks inside through Morteza's window. He then turns towards Morteza.

'Dear old man! This new stuff is for young people. Just take a drag of your good old gear.'

Morteza doesn't understand that the soldier is referring to drugs and simply says, 'Yes, sir.' The light of the flashlight falls over his hair.

'You seem like a cool guy. You've got highlights in your hair. I like you. You can go now.'

Morteza starts driving.

'All's good, Doctor. You can now come around.'

Mosaddegh laughs and shakes his head.

'This is Tehran?! I've been underground for a long time, it seems! Good thing they didn't arrest you. Otherwise, you'd be accused of trafficking antiques!'

Morteza laughs out loud. They reach a side street. He stops the truck in front of a building.

'I have something urgent to take care of here. You're not in a hurry, are you?'

Mosaddegh chuckles.

'I was underground for eighty-seven years and will soon be going back right there. I'm in no rush at all. You go do what you need to do.'

Morteza reaches into the glove compartment. He pulls out Maliheh's nightgown and unfolds it. Mosaddegh's gaze is on Morteza's hands. The photo frame and the knife appear through the gown. Morteza gives the frame to Mosaddegh.

'This is Maliheh!'

Mosaddegh's eyes move from the photograph to the gown and the knife Morteza is holding in his hands. He turns around and looks outside through the passenger window.

'The gown,' Mosaddegh begins, 'you not being around for thirty years, the picture of Maliheh whom you say was your wife, the something urgent you need to take care of, and you holding a knife in your hand, the combination of all of these tells me you're up to settling personal scores. Didn't you say the National Party?! That party and I have always underlined just one thing: the rule of law. We are not here for personal rulings or enforcements, but for the law, my dear man. The law.'

Morteza turns towards his own window.

This seems like a dream. I have loved Mosaddegh for my whole life and now I'm sitting here with him in my truck. I have a knife in my hand, he has a photograph in his. He says, 'Law', I say, 'Knife'. Which law, my dear Doctor? These men have sold the whole country and brought in hired guns. I waited 30 years to do what I need to do in this jungle, no, not a jungle, in this lawless dusty desert.

Mosaddegh turns to Morteza.

'You old man! Why did you come to me the very first day after your release? I don't know you, and you don't owe me anything. If you still keep Mosaddegh in your mind, it's because surrounded by all those mercenaries, I stood there and asked for the rule of law. Now, call it a jungle or a desert. A hand and a weapon, without the rule of law, mean nothing but trouble. There you go. Now, it's between you, the knife, and the building. But I hope when you come back out of the building, your knife is not bloody. I'm going to sit right here and look at you and Maliheh's laughter in this picture. May you be safe.'

Mosaddegh holds his walking stick in one hand and the picture frame in the other. Morteza leans towards him. He places a kiss on the hand holding the walking stick and gets out of the truck. Mosaddegh rests his head on the handle of the walking stick.

Morteza buzzes the door. A woman asks who it is. Morteza says he is one of Haji's friends and has a package for him. After a moment, a light shines through the diamond-shaped glass window of the door and it opens. Morteza walks in. A huge chandelier hangs from the high ceiling over the snaking staircase. He rushes up the stairs. The woman is standing at the top of the stairs. Morteza reaches her. She is carrying a tray with a bowl of half-finished soup on it. She seems to be the maid. She says hello, and Morteza asks which room is Haji's. The woman is alarmed by Morteza's behaviour. She wants to take the package from him and deliver it herself. Calmly, Morteza puts his hand in his pocket, pulls out the knife, and presses the switchblade's safety lock. He holds the knife under the woman's throat.

'As long as you remain silent, the sharpness of this knife won't hurt your veins. Otherwise, my hand is quick, and this knife pretty sharp. Get going now. When we go into the room, you're going to sit there in a corner like a good girl and watch it all. Come on, get moving!'

Terrified, the woman walks towards a door, opens it, and enters. Morteza follows her into the room and locks the door.

You follow the woman into the room and lock the door.

I

follow the woman into the room and lock the door. The room is half dark. The curtains are pulled. There is only one table lamp on.

Your gaze goes from the woman to the bed where someone is lying.

I gesture with my head for the woman to sit down.

Scared, the woman sits down on the chair. You walk towards the bed. You stop. Your gaze, my gaze, examines the man lying on the bed. He is old. There is an oxygen tank and an IV drip hanger next to the bed. The man's eyes are open. Terrified, he looks at you without saying a word. You don't know where to start. Where should I start? From the night of the 15th of Mehr, 1401,[13] when the two of us were sitting on the couch, half of our attention on the movie playing, and the rest on the news. Who was arrested? Who were the prisoners whose locations were known and who were those who disappeared? How many were killed? Whose corpse was confiscated and their family threatened? Which family had secretly moved their loved one's body to their house, asking around, among neighbours, for ice to cover the corpse and keep it fresh until they could give it a proper clandestine burial? Which families could then take their fresh grief back home with them, to never forgive, to never forget?

★

It was past midnight when the door buzzer went off. The fear raised by the sound filled our eyes. I took our mobile phones to the closet and hid them in the pocket of the black suit from our wedding night. You slipped the laptop under the TV stand. The buzzing wouldn't stop. Then came the sound of punches and kicks. On the intercom monitor, I saw several men. One of them climbed up onto the gate and then we heard him jumping down into the front yard. The lights in the house were off. I ran towards you. I embraced you. I said, 'Maliheh! It's nothing. Don't worry. They are after me.' You embraced me and told me they were rather there for you. The way they were invading the house, I knew they were coming for both of us. The front yard gate was opened; a flock of men were at the building's door. They were turning the doorknob; it was locked. Someone kicked at the door, and the lock broke. The first man came in. He had a gun and held it pointed towards you. The end credits music of the film was playing when the second man entered. He flipped the light switch. Then two other men entered. Before you could protest, the first man knocked you in the face with his gun grip. You fell on the couch. When you tried to run towards me screaming, another man pulled you from your hair which you had just cut a few days before and threw you over to the corner.

When you tried to get up from the couch to help me, the first man put his knee over your throat and held his gun to your forehead. He said that if you made a scene, he would hang both of us revolutionary losers from our butts. The other two men were busy searching the house.

One of them shouted, 'Where's your phone, you whore?' You didn't answer, just kept gritting your teeth. Your eyes were on me and on the man's knee on my throat.

While a knee was over your throat, one of the men slapped me in the face. He grabbed me from the back of my neck and pushed me to the wall.

Your muffled scream filled the room, and the pressure from the knee over your throat increased as the man's hand started to move down between your legs. The man grabbed your balls in his hands and pulled. Your eyes turned to the man whom everyone called Haji, and, in pain, you noticed the blue colour of his eyes and the mark of a thick lumpy scar on his left cheek. The man had his hands in my bra and in between my legs, looking for my mobile phone. We heard the wardrobe in the bedroom falling with a crash, the cabinet doors in the kitchen opening and the plates breaking on the floor tiles. Finally, one of the men came out with two mobile phones in his hand and another pulled out the laptop from under the TV stand.

There were two cars in the street, a white Peugeot and a silver Citroën Xantia. They put me in the Xantia, and you screamed out to the neighbours for help, but they had all turned their lights off and looked at the scene discreetly through their windows.

You shouted, 'Maliheh, don't be afraid. They can't do anything to you.' A hand grabbed your head and as it was trying to push you in the car, your right eyebrow hit the top edge of the door frame and was torn open. I could see blood running down the white paint of the car, red drops falling to the ground, lit by the streetlights. The blue-eyed man sat next to me and ordered the Xantia driver to start moving. Tyre screeches echoed through the night. You screamed, calling me Malih instead of Maliheh, and I turned around to look through the rear window but before I could get to the 'r' in 'Morteza', Haji pulled my hair and pushed my head down between my legs.

I was screaming 'Malih! Malih!' when someone elbowed me in my temple. I lost consciousness. When I opened my eyes, I was in solitary confinement. Then came the interrogations and insomnia. The accusations were already written down on paper, waiting for my signature, but my only utterance was to ask about Maliheh's whereabouts. I asked the same question in court and then simply stood there silent.

Two months later, you learned of my death and for a week you did not touch your food. You did not cry either, simply stared at the wall, reviewing the past and the path we had taken together, up to the night of the attack, our pursuit of ideals, freedom, reforms, everything we had spent our youth on, only to question them all once you arrived at the news of my death.

The cause of death was declared as suicide by jumping from a height. I never believed it. When, for lack of food and extreme weakness, I lost consciousness, they took me to the prison infirmary. There, the doctor on call who had recently been transferred there from the mortuary told me that the truth was not what I had been told. I learned that your body had been found off of Qazvin Road near Abik Cement Factory. A body that showed signs of beatings and rape, signs of asphyxiation around the neck. I don't know where the scream I let out that night in the infirmary came from. The young doctor injected me with a tranquiliser to help me fall asleep. When I woke up in the prison ward, the only thing in front of my eyes was a pair of blue eyes, eyes that remained with me everywhere I went from then on. When I was sentenced to execution and when the appeals court changed the ruling to 30 years, they were right there in front of me. All those 30 years, I exercised and punched the wall to not let old age conquer me. My hair turned white the very first month. In the mirror, I looked at the young old man I was, his right eyebrow split in two, his eyes filled with tearful sorrow swallowed whole – a man who kept stacking anger upon anger until the day he would be set free. I had found the name and address of the man to whom those blue eyes belonged. I waited for the day I would leave the prison and arrive here and ask him all there was to ask, to use this very switchblade to pull out of his throat the 30 years of you not being here and the 30 years of my own lost life. I should learn all about that night and bring this night to an end.

When the car turned into a side street, I looked up. I could see the monstrous factory in the distance and its lights shining. The car proceeded on the dirt road, and, terrified, I could say nothing. There was only silence. At the end of the side road and amid the darkness, the car came to a stop. The driver got out, started walking in the light emanating from the car and lit a cigarette. I turned towards the man. The blue of his eyes was visible even in the dark. He reached into my shirt and ripped it open all the way down. I screamed. He slapped me in the face. In my first attempt to fight, he locked my arms and legs and lay me on the seat. Before I could scream again to ask for help, he slapped me a second time. He then pulled his trouser zipper down and threw himself over me. He spread my legs and got going. One of his hands was over my mouth, preventing my muffled screams to reach even the roof of the car. When he finished, he said, 'Now you carry my sperm. Maybe this very sperm can ask for God's grace and save you in the other world.' The door on my side opened. The driver threw a rope around my neck and dragged me out. I kept kicking, staring at the blue-eyed man who was pulling his zipper up. My eyes were bulging out of their sockets. I ran short of breath and everything turned black.

Morteza is squatting, holding his head between his hands, swallowing his pain. He gets up. He pulls out the closed knife from his pocket and presses the safety button. The silver blade shines under the light of the table lamp. His gaze meets the man's. The blue eyes of the man with an old scar on his cheek are filled with death. Morteza's are filled with blood. His face is flushed with rage. The maid gets up from her chair.

'Sir, dear, this man is sick and all alone. His children have left Iran and he is alive only thanks to this oxygen tank. I don't know what has happened in the past, and why you, a stranger I don't know, are here. But forgive him. Forgive this half-dead man.'

Morteza holds the knife's blade on the man's throat. The man closes his eyes.

'Morteza!'

Morteza turns around. Maliheh stands on the other side of the bed. Morteza straightens his back. Standing on his side of the bed, he looks at her.

'Yes, my love!'

Maliheh reaches out with her hand. Morteza too extends his hand. Their palms touch, their fingers locking, caressing one another. Maliheh has stayed young; Morteza's hair has turned white. Maliheh's eyes are anxious; Morteza's are covered with a veil of tears. Not blinking, he fills his eyes up with Maliheh. A drop of blood falls from his eyebrow. Maliheh's other hand extends and cleans the old scar on his eyebrow that has burst open again. She runs her bloody finger over her lips. A smile appears on her crimson lips. Morteza asks her for her bloody finger. Maliheh's hand touches Morteza's lips. He kisses her bloody finger. Maliheh brings down her hand and takes the knife from Morteza. She presses the button, folds the blade, and lays it in its sheath.

'Dr Mosaddegh is waiting for you downstairs!'

Morteza takes the closed knife from her and looks at it. He turns to the blue-eyed man whose gaze is fixed at the ceiling, his tears finding their way away from the corner of his eyes. Morteza notices a plastic bag full of urine by the bed. He turns to the maid.

'He's pissed himself out of fear.'

He puts the switchblade in his pocket. His hand dangles in mid-air. There is no sign of Maliheh anymore. He pulls his hand back and pushes the blanket covering the man away. The catheter has shifted out of place and the whole bed is wet with urine. The man's weak body has sunken into the mattress. Morteza bends over him.

'Too bad there's no God, or else I'd ask him to save you. I spit on your half-dead soul and on the surviving vultures around you, all of whom are going to be sent to hell by a seventy-year-old white-haired shadow starting tomorrow. So get used to just suffering here until you die, you filthy, pissing bastard!'

He unlocks the doors and heads out of the room.

Now I can go lose myself. Your memory has turned into a set of eyes, eyes watching over me from above. Not giving a damn about the bloodstain over my eyebrow, not wiping away the veil of tears from my eyes, I reach the bottom of the stairs and see myself in the diamond-shaped glass of the door that has turned into a mirror. I finally wipe the tears away and step outside. You leap down from your position up above me and, through the half-open door not yet shut by the last push of its hinge, you too burst out.

The truck is right there. You push the tarpaulin aside and through the shattered corner of the coffin, you see the skull of Dr Mosaddegh, who looks at you through empty sockets. Dr Mosaddegh's voice fills your ears: 'My dear, we should leave before it gets light!' You pull the fabric over the coffin, sit at the wheel, and look at the empty space left behind by Dr Mosaddegh on the passenger seat. Only our picture frame and my nightgown remain on the passenger seat now, and the walking stick, leaning against the door. You start the truck. In your mind, you review the directions to Ebn-e Babviyeh Cemetery. You turn on the stereo. Qamar's voice fills the truck cabin, and you start whispering 'The Bird of Dawn' with her. You shift into gear, and the eight-cylinder truck tears off the gravel with its tyres screeching. I am left standing there under the streetlight, knowing that a checkpoint awaits you by the first turn and that you will step on the gas and speed up, shift up, and pass straight through it without stopping. I, too, will make my way to Ebn-e Babviyeh through another path. Which one of us will get there first?

Notes

1. Ahmad Abad village, in Alborz province, where Mohammad Mosaddegh spent his years of exile after the coup in his estates. He was buried there in the living room of his house.
2. Haji is a Muslim man who has completed the Hajj pilgrimage, but it is also commonly used to refer to anyone. Some people, especially if not religious, might find this form of address disrespectful.
3. 19 August, 1953.
4. The 21 July Uprising of 1952.
5. A traditional, highly absorbent, red cotton fabric (often with a striped or grid pattern) used for drying and cleaning in Iran, similar to traditional Turkish towels.
6. 1979.
7. Seyyed Abol-Ghasem Kashani (1882-1962), Shiite cleric and politician who played a major role in the 1953 coup against Prime Minister Mosaddegh.
8. 16 September, 2022.
9. Fazlollah Zahedi (1892-1963), Iranian military officer and statesman, who replaced Prime Minister Mosaddegh after the coup, serving from 1953-1955.
10. A short black-and-white video from August 1953, released

by the CIA in 2013, shows Mosaddegh's house following the coup – the destruction of the buildings around the house, protestors around the house, and several officials visiting the house, including General Zahedi and Seyyed Kashani.

11. Qamar-ol-Moluk Vaziri (1905-1959), celebrated Iranian singer, the first woman of her era to sing in public without wearing a veil and among the first Iranian singers who recorded on the gramophone.

12. A form of Persian music, considered as equivalent to the ballad.

13. 7 October, 2022, during the Woman, Life, Freedom revolutionary uprising.

A Suspended Spectre in the Tehran Sky

Navid Hamzavi

IN THE BBC RADIO 1953 archive, a voice reads the following line in the midday news: 'A man threw himself out of the third-floor window of a mansion in Tehran and remained suspended in the air...'

The audio tape is choppy and undated. The same line has appeared on other archives, referring to separate events, but again damaged. Whether the tape is defective, or the news is censored is not discernible. The account is more comprehensive in the archives of the years 1963 and 1979. For instance, in the news script of the year 1963, the presenter mentions a cypress tree in front of the third-floor window. By juxtaposing the dates in the archives, determining the location of the incident, and referring to historical texts, it is possible to arrive at a narrative that, if not definitive, is more comprehensive.

To give an example, on page 323 of the first volume of *Suspicious Political Deaths in Iran*[1] this exact line is repeated. Determining the accurate time of the event is not possible. Either the date of the incident has been distorted, or the event is related not to one person but to several different men who have thrown themselves out of the window at different times and remained suspended in the air.

If you follow one of the narratives through archival texts, political memoirs, the BBC Radio archive, and oral history recordings, and take a walk towards the intersection of Heshmat al-Doleh Square on the afternoon of mid-August 1953 in Kaj Street, Tehran, Iran, the reflection of a horrendous sound makes the cobblestone beneath the feet tremble, and if the sunlight allows you to look upwards, you see the body of a man suspended, between the sky and the earth, in front of the third-floor window of the mansion. Tiny shards of glass surround him, making a sacred halo as the sunlight reflects on the fragmented pieces. Blood gushes out from his hands and fingers, dangling in the air, never reaching the ground. The suspended man lingers between life and death; blood spurts out of the corners of his mouth and the gash on his forehead, yet he does not die. He must confront death, and yet he does not.

I ascend the stairs, I pass through the corridor, traverse the hallway, and enter the room: light, shattered glass, blood specks spattered on the floor. Two men stand in the centre of the room, gazing through the frame of the window, where the body of a man is suspended outside. The window frame is ornately designed. I ask, 'Why don't you let him fall?' One of the men says, 'Everyone should see what the English have done to us,' and explains that if it weren't for these blue eyes, he wouldn't be there now, casting his gaze at the half-lifeless body of the suspended man.

'But years have passed since today,' I say. 'Let him die. He's suffering.' He resents my words. 'Believe me,' I go on. 'Just look at yourself in the mirror; you've aged.'

'I haven't seen myself in the mirror for years,' he says. I pause and look imploringly at the other man, hoping he might intervene.

'This issue needs to be raised with the British,' he says, as if he can't speak to the first man, or doesn't want to, like they are separated by great distances from each other.

I step out of the room, pass through the corridor, and reach the stairs, which spiral downwards, their end not in sight. The steps coil into each other like a whirlpool. Looking down from the top, it feels like I'm sinking. It takes years to descend the stairs. Reaching the bottom of them, being out on the street, right beneath the body of a man suspended in front of the third-floor window, I greet a crowd chanting protest slogans. From their wrath, I can tell it is June 1963. Security forces fire into the sky, one or two bullets lodge in the tree, leaves scatter in the air, falling under the feet of the protesters. A youthful journalist is crafting a report for a London newspaper. Between his fingers, fragments of the report can be seen:

'...A man threw himself out of the third-floor window of a mansion in Tehran and remained suspended in the air... Iranians hold Great Britain responsible for the crime... Protesters say they no longer need English advisors... and that public and private spaces, homes, and libraries should be cleansed of colonial elements...'

I ascend the stairs, I pass through the corridor, traverse the hallway, and enter the room: light, shattered glass, blood specks spattered on the floor. Two men stand in the centre of the room, gazing through the frame of the window, where the body of a man is suspended outside. One of the men is wearing a grey robe, a brown cloak over the robe, and a black turban on his head. His beard meets the cusp of his throat. I approach the fractured window. The man with the turban says: 'Careful with the blood, do not get *Najis*[2].' I look down. It must be 1963 as the crowd is still chanting slogans, leaves are falling, and a young man is crafting a report for a London newspaper. My eyes fall upon the suspended man. The signs of his imminent death are evident. I say to the man with the turban, 'Let him fall; he is nearing his end, let him be laid to rest with dignity. You too should offer a burial prayer over his body, so that this chapter concludes well.'

He furrows his brows and shouts: 'What are you saying, sir? This crime of the enemies of Islam should be framed, not buried in the ground!' Sitting himself down in front of the *rehal,*[3] he asks me to pass the Quran to him. I ask the other man in the room, who is taller and closer to the bookshelves. He takes down the Quran, which is resting on a brown wooden shelf, the highest shelf in the library. Handling the book delicately, he brings it close to his face, kisses its spine, touches it with his forehead, and gently, with respect, as if cradling a fragile, mysterious orb, places the book in my hands. I pass the book to the man with the turban. He, too, brings the Quran close to his face, kisses its spine, touches it with his forehead, and gently, with respect, as if cradling a fragile, mysterious orb, places the book on the *rehal* and starts to recite. There is another book on the bookshelves, whose origins can be traced back to an article published on the BBC Persian website. The article recounts the memories of the other man in the room regarding his views on the man with the turban. The memoir, in fact, is a compilation of notes and recollections by the other man in the room, published under the title *The Ahistorical Cycle*[4] in which he refers to the man with the turban as a British agent. The second paragraph of page 223, which is reiterated verbatim on the BBC Persian website, reads: 'I swear on the Quran that he is a puppet of the British.' My gaze passes from the library to the suspended man; blood has trickled from the corner of his mouth and hangs in the air.

I step out of the room, pass through the corridor, and reach the stairs, which spiral downwards, their end not in sight. The steps coil into each other like a whirlpool. It takes years to descend them and reach the street. An enraged crowd, like the horses of a chariot galloping on the sands of an ancient land, come charging towards me, chasing a fiery column. Heavily-built men are running after a woman who's been set on fire, and who runs in turn from the fire inside her body and the chariot wheels of their masculinity. A man howls, 'Westernised whore!' as he slams his clenched fists into the woman's jaw. The woman's screams smell of charred meat. The smoke plume from the burning woman and the swirling dust kicked up by the chariot wheels entwine and reach the man suspended in front of the third-floor window of the mansion.

I ascend the stairs, I pass through the corridor, traverse the hallway, and enter the room: light, shattered glass, blood specks spattered on the floor. Two men stand in the centre of the room, gazing through the frame of the window, where the body of a man is suspended outside. The dry creak of the door breaks the turbaned man's train of thought. If every moment is approached calmly and slowly, details come to life, and the thoughts of the turbaned man, scattered in the dispersed dust, materialise and become apparent in the room's space...

This time calmly and slowly:

I ascend the stairs. The footsteps' echo fills the spiral staircase. On the wall of the corridor I am about to pass through, a calendar displays the year 1979 adorned with Islamic patterns. The clock pendulum swings calmly and slowly. I nudge the door ajar. The slowness of the moment does not break the turbaned man's train of thought. The outline of his thoughts materialise in the particles of dust suspended in the light; he is raping a woman... A woman with blue eyes who does not speak Persian... she pleads in vain...

I ascend the stairs, I pass through the corridor, traverse the hallway, and enter the room: light, shattered glass, blood specks spattered on the floor. Two men stand in the centre of the room, gazing through the frame of the window, where the body of a man is suspended outside. The dry creak of the door breaks the turbaned man's train of thought. The man is seated behind the *rehal*. The smell of the woman's charred flesh fills the room. I say, now that your prayers have been answered and Islam has triumphed, allow the suspended body of the man to fall. Let's bathe, scent, shroud, and pray over the body, and finally, after all these years, lay it to rest in the ground. The turban man says, 'Haste is the devil's work,' then raises his head from the book and fixes his gaze on the western horizon.

The other man leans in, whispering in my ear, 'The British and Americans did their job; I have to go.'

'Stay,' I say. 'Perhaps we can resolve the issue through dialogue.'

'But the problem won't be solved here,' he says. 'I need to get in touch with the Westerners as soon as possible.'

I step out of the room, pass through the corridor, and reach the stairs, which spiral downwards, their end not in sight. The steps coil into each other like a whirlpool. It takes years to descend them and reach the street. It must have been decades since the crowd first stood with clenched fists, shouting slogans at the body of a man suspended between the earth and the sky, in front of a third-floor window. I probe and inquire. Concerns are growing over the presence of foreigners on the third floor of the building. Three or four foreigners have come to visit the suspended man. On the newstands, along the eastern side of the street, under the cypress trees, headlines summarise what's being talked about inside the building in bold black print. A newspaper, with a sidebar dedicated to the daily prayer times, announces: 'Westerners have taken full responsibility for the 1953 Iranian coup.' Another headline declares: 'The Western scandal has been laid bare.' On the cover of a magazine: 'One word: the West is to blame.' Guards at the front of the building have been instructed not to allow anyone to enter. A man in the crowd cries out, 'Our honour is at stake.' A collective echo follows: 'Our honour is at stake.' The fluctuating frequency of the chants vibrates the suspended man's body.

I ascend the stairs, I pass through the corridor, traverse the hallway, and enter the room: light, shattered glass, blood specks spattered on the floor. Two men stand in the centre of the room, gazing through the frame of the window, where the body of a man is suspended, caught between the earth and the sky. A handful of foreigners are talking to the turbaned man, sitting opposite them at the *rehal*. Seated on the ground, they cover their noses with handkerchiefs. The room is filled with a stale stench. They have come to mediate, in hopes the suspended man can be brought down and laid to rest. Sweating with shame, the foreigners continuously criticise themselves, as if confessing their sins to a priest. Segments of this conversation can be located in the archives of the University of St Andrews, Scotland, in the collection titled 'Groundbreaking Conversations'.[5] The archive is accessible to students and professors across the UK and has recently been equipped with keyword-search capabilities. This brief description – which is best found by entering the keywords 'Quran' and 'Iran' – mentions that during the conversation, the turbaned man suddenly rises from behind the *rehal* and exits the room. This behaviour, which seemed a bit strange and disrespectful to the foreign delegation, was explained by the Iranian translator as due to the arrival of prayer time. The author of the report, who apparently had some familiarity with the Persian language, also notes that the translator approached the turbaned man and asked him, now that the foreign delegation had bravely come to Iran and confessed their sins, to let the suspended man fall. The Groundbreaking Conversations archive quotes the author as saying: 'The man with the turban frowns in frustration. The translator says to him, "Look at yourself, your beard has turned grey; you've grown old."The man with the turban pulls on his cloak, curses Satan, murmurs something in Arabic, and says to the translator: "He must remain suspended as a reminder of what they have done to us. He must remain suspended so that we might distinguish between right and wrong.'"

Another man in the room is being interviewed by a Western media outlet. I hear him say, 'Instead of engaging with me, these foreigners are playing footsie with this non-Iranian,' referring to the man with the turban. I can't help but say that, as far as I know, he too is Iranian.

It's as if my voice has reached him from a great distance, and he shouts back at me, 'Do you know what you are saying?'

I say to the foreigners, 'Your apologetic presence worsens the situation.' I point to the wall and add, 'Look, since you arrived, the window's decorative frame has disappeared! Now, they don't even catch each other's eye by accident. Allow them to face death, come to terms with themselves, and let this suspended man fall.'

'We are here for precisely this reason,' one of the foreigners replies. 'Nonetheless, we want you to know that we respect your culture. Our reporter is even going to prepare a report on *Andaruni*[6] in Iranian architecture.'

I step out of the room, pass through the corridor, and reach the stairs, which spiral downwards, their end not in sight. The steps coil into each other like a whirlpool. It takes years to descend them and reach the street. The scent of women's bodies eclipses the stench of the suspended man's body. Their intense fragrance suggests that it must be the autumn of 2022. One of the women on the street shouts, 'We must bring down the suspended man!' The security forces turn their guns on her, taking aim at her forehead. The woman's hair is thrown back, blood trickles down from her arched brows. The woman's body is handed over. A girl reaches up to the feet of the suspended man, crying out, 'Pull him down!' The security forces aim straight between the girl's eyes; blood pours down her face, her hair, her shoulders, pooling at her feet. Three young girls run towards the foot of the mansion's staircase. The security forces open fire. Blood cascades down the building's stone steps onto the landing.

I climb the stairs. Bloodstains form on the steps. I pass through the corridor, traverse the hallway, and enter the room: light, shattered glass, blood specks spattered on the floor. Two men are struggling to keep the suspended man from falling. Both are nervous and trembling. The lines on their faces and bodies quiver, appearing and disappearing. They take on absurd shapes. At times, pieces of their bodies break off, turn to dust, and disperse into the air. It must still be autumn, 2022, or the second half of that year, as the smell of blood is still wafting through the room, and the struggle over the hanging man continues.

I step out of the room, pass through the corridor, and reach the stairs, which spiral downwards, their end not in sight. The steps coil into each other like a whirlpool. I will reach the street in the future. Perhaps in the year 2053. I wonder, when I step onto the street, will a man have thrown himself out of the third-floor window of a mansion in Tehran, and be suspended in the air?

Perhaps he won't be there anymore. Perhaps the blood will no longer dangle between the sky and the earth. Perhaps the soft light will carry the dappled shadows of the trees, unhindered, onto the pavement of the street.

Perhaps the ornate frame of the window will have been restored. And the suspended man will have met his maker, his funeral rites having been performed and his body laid to rest. Perhaps the two men inside the room, having nothing left to gaze upon, will have turned to dust, and dispersed into the air.

Or perhaps, within the archive of audio, visual, and written records, other suspended bodies will have materialised in the Tehran sky, their shadows having multiplied, casting a heavy weight over the crowds, obstructing the slanting rays of light in this future.

Perhaps the two men, now ancient and decrepit, have become rooted to the floor of the room, the body of the suspended man having transformed into a sacred idol, to be invoked and repeated, time and again, in the face of any enemy. And perhaps the mansion has been filled with the old stench of decay and blood.

I will reach the street in the future. Perhaps in 2053. I will step through the doorframe, pass through the corridor, and reach the stairs, which spiral downwards, their end not in sight.

Notes

1. Smith, 1999, *Suspicious Political Deaths in Iran*, Liverpool University Press, Liverpool
2. In Islamic law, *najis* are things or people regarded as ritually unclean. there are two kinds of najis: inherent and acquired.
3. An X-shaped, foldable bookrest used to hold religious scriptures.
4. A.A, 1982, *The Ahistorical Cycle*, Hachette, Paris
5. Tera, Amy. 'A Souvenir from Iran'. 30 August 1990. 'Groundbreaking Conversations' Collection. SAN.1990.007, Box 1, Folder 3. University of St Andrews, Scotland.
6. In traditional Persian residential architecture, the *Andaruni* is a part of the house in which the private quarters are established, where the women of the house are free to move about without being seen by an outsider.

The Blaze of Abadan

Naseem Jamnia

*NEW SOURCE OF URANIUM FOUND IN OIL
DEPOSITS NEAR PERSIAN GULF*
Iran Worldwide, dated June 2051

THE SOUTHWESTERN CITY OF Abadan in the oil-rich Khuzestan province may soon find new purpose in uranium mining, the Iranian Department of Energy announced yesterday.

Although Abadan once provided 25% of the country's fuel needs, the shift to nuclear energy with the 2031 Directive on Transition to Sustainable Energy during the Interim Government has devastated the city's – and region's – economy. Today, it is one of the poorest provinces of Iran, with an increase in child illiteracy and gang violence after the recent Pahlavi administration pulled support in favour of focused urbanisation. Yet Abadan might regain the country's attention with a source of mineable uranium a mere 70 kilometres from the city.

Under the Pahlavi administration of 2032, Iran's Department of Energy had initiated a survey for potential new sources of uranium to aid the country's transition to nuclear energy, but it was not until relations with China, Iran's primary source of imported uranium concentrate, soured under the subsequent 2048 Pahlavi administration that a concerted effort was made to find native deposits.

'What makes Abadan an ideal location,' says Shirin Dameneh, Director of Energy, 'is it already has infrastructure from its oil days – albeit severely damaged from Cyclone Khosrow in 2050. This is the perfect opportunity to pivot Abadan towards uranium mining and maintain access to multiple storage facilities. Local officials have been cooperative and are just as eager to explore the potential of this deposit and bring Abadan back to its glory days.'

Khuzestan Province has faced severe droughts the last several decades. The 2036 Pahlavi administration declared a majority of the province inhospitable when adding Khuzestan to its climate refugee relocation program. The 2049 motion to designate the desertified regions around Haftgel in the central part of the province as a nuclear waste site, pushed forth by then-minority Morality Party leader Mohammad Amin Bagherzadeh, initially sparked controversy despite being passed by majority vote. In light of upcoming and continued surveys of the region, a series of energy summits have been planned over the next fourteen months.

★

Twenty-One Days until the Blaze

As usual, the Khuzestan Majles went in circles. I massaged the bone around my eye prosthetic, a dull ache pulsing behind the abused socket.

'As God wills it,' I said, 'business is business.'

Ahvazi, who thought themself more important than the rest of us (since Ahvaz had once been the centre of the province, back when our country was held together with more than Scotch tape and prayer), glared at me. 'Try saying that when it's *your* jurisdiction being flooded with bi gheirat Tehranis who want to exploit our resources.'

Only Ahvazi would give a shit about honour when there's money at stake.

'Pedar-sagha have already gentrified Abadan,' I said. 'What, you think that because our operations are underground, we aren't feeling the ramifications of the discovery? Legitimate money in the city means the government will allow us to keep more in our own pockets.' Money that resulted from our oil operations, and which kept my people fed. The refineries may have officially been shuttered over a decade ago, but that hadn't stopped me.

What did I care for a drying climate and a dying earth, if it meant the people under my care could live? *Nuclear* was a word for the wealthy. Nuclear wasn't even a dream for the poor.

'Since when do those kos kholha operate on fairness?' said Shushtari, burly arms crossed, that ridiculous moustache of his twitching. 'More money in the city means more money for *them*. They'll never look at an Arab and deal fairly.'

The implications about my ethnicity landed. 'Goh tu dahanet,' I spat. 'I'm more Lur than you!'

'Abadani,' said Ahvazi wearily, who had as many Arabs in their domain as I did in mine. 'Can you not start a fight for *once*?'

'I'm not trying to start a fight. I'm trying to keep the lights on and my people alive and fed. And succeeding, unlike some at this table too focused on our "glorious past".'

Shushtari, whom everyone knew wanted a return to monarchy despite nearly a century without it (as if our presidents for decades hadn't been Pahlavis anyway), slapped the table and glared at me. I'd seen tougher stares from donkeys. 'Listen, madar-jendeh—'

Beside me, my late sister's child — no longer a child — choked on their tea at that gravest of insults. Roshan pressed their face into their elbow as they coughed, interrupting Shushtari's tirade, and I patted their thigh. I'd taken to bringing Roshan to these meetings so I could lessen the work expected from my right hand, Sohaila.

Roshan's shoulders shook – they were laughing. Silly dear.

'Ya Ali madad,' muttered Izehi, a woman of few words but ample faith. 'Azizan, please. We have but three weeks before the officials come to tour the proposed site for the new complex. That is three weeks to organise. A grand protest is surely our best bet. They cannot push our people out in favour of their own.'

Ahvazi perked up. Like Izehi, they had too much confidence in our young democracy. 'If we can mobilise our populations, get them to Abadan before the tour, we can stage a demonstration the likes of which haven't been seen since the Jina Revolts.'

Bitterness flooded my mouth. The Jina Revolts hadn't become the Jina Revolution until after the last ayatollah had died. Now the morde shur's mentee was in office, claiming he'd set the country back to moral rights.

As if reading my mind, Roshan muttered, 'Like peaceful protest has ever worked,' too quiet for anyone else to hear.

Shushtari, though, gave my nibling a thoughtful look.

Ahvazi looked around to the others for confirmation of the plan. The little lamb newly in charge of Bandar Mahshahr nodded, while the old goat ruling Ramhormoz far past when he should have retired, only grunted. (I wasn't convinced he hadn't fallen asleep as we'd argued.)

The area around my eye throbbed again. Were they forgetting how little the Water Riots of '46 had changed? How few resources were sent when Cyclones Bahareh, Khosrow, and most recently Sepideh, hit our province? An area that had once been almost five million people had fractured; our cities had bloated and countryside emptied of all those able to flee – some to Tehran and Shiraz and Esfahan, others leaving Iran altogether – until we were down to three million across Khuzestan. Thirty counties had been reduced to six.

'Fine,' I bit out. 'By all means, flood my streets with interlocutors. I'm sure that'll solve the issue.'

The meeting thus adjourned, I hobbled out, my lower back twinging with the pain of sitting for so long. Outside, I was surprised to see Sohaila waiting among the other members of our various factions.

Roshan had not joined us yet, so I pulled her aside. 'Yes?'

Lips in a line, she handed me a note. 'This came from Homayun.'

Homayun was my most reliable plant in the official Abadan municipal offices. God help me, but working with those pedar-sagha irritated me to no end. Most of them men, but some of them women – all of them looked at me with disgust and did not hide their disdain. I made no apologies for who I was: not for the eye I lost protesting their former masters, not for the women I'd long welcomed into my bed, and not for loving Abadan more than they could ever understand.

I skimmed the page, then cursed under my breath. My right hand, always a stern woman, looked impassive, but I could see the worry she hid well. 'This changes things,' she murmured. 'What are you going to do?'

I crushed the note. I'd need to burn it, lest it fall into the wrong hands. 'I suppose it's time to visit the mine.'

★

MEET THE GRADUATES

Excerpted Interview with Roshan Etezadi, A.M. 2050

THE MAROON: Do you have plans to visit Iran to continue your research?

ETEZADI: Well, things are a little up in the air right now. My mother and I had been planning to visit, but that's been put on hold. But the trip was personal in nature – she left during the Jina Revolts in the twenties and hasn't been back since. I've never been, either.

THE MAROON: Do you still have family in Iran?

ETEZADI: My mother's sister is her last remaining family, and she lives in one of the southwestern cities. The province she lives in has been pretty decimated by cyclones, the most recent being [Cyclone] Khosrow three months ago, so local infrastructure has been heavily damaged and travel has been tricky. Our plan was to fly to Kuwait and take a boat. I suppose once we got there, we probably would have gotten involved in the relief efforts. My mother is a recovering academic [*laugh*] – she's been working with the Center for Human Rights in Iran for over a decade. Well, had been, before she got sick.

THE MAROON: That's fascinating – so your mother was involved in human rights work. Did that, or your heritage, play a part in your research interests?

ETEZADI: Both did, absolutely. It felt pretty straightforward to combine my interest in climate catastrophe with my homeland. Iran's been undergoing rapid desertification over the past three, four decades. The transition to renewable energy under the Interim Government was only country-wide on paper. The nuclear power plants that had once been such a source of fear for the West have been the country's main energy source for the last fifteen years or so. However, as we've seen around the world, poorer communities are unable to afford the switch to sustainable energy and still rely on fossil fuels. Plus, Iran's economy was based on oil for arguably over a century. I have no doubt they have a hand in the continued use of fossil fuels around the world.

THE MAROON: It's funny you call it your homeland, since you've never been.

ETEZADI: [*pause*] Well, maybe not, but it's always… called to me.

THE MAROON: You were born in the United States, correct? Do you consider yourself a third-culture kid?

ETEZADI: That's… one way to put it. I think many children of immigrants understand the straddling of multiple cultures and the feeling of never quite belonging to any of them. Some people handle it with grace. It's been a struggle for me to figure out where I belong. I'm honestly a little nervous that in going to Iran, I'll find I don't belong there, either.

THE MAROON: Surely your aunt will take you in.

ETEZADI: I'm sure she will. I think she does a lot of boots-on-the-ground work herself, so I figure, whenever we do manage to go, I'll get involved with her work. Who knows? Maybe I can help the diaspora get more involved, too. Maybe being born on the outside will help bring valuable perspective. What I do know is that despite the changes the country's undergone over the last thirty years, things haven't changed *enough*. The Jina Party hasn't gained the foothold many people had hoped, and instead, we're seeing the children of the old monarchy fight it out with the children of the old Islamic regime. [*Editor's note: The Jina Party is the common name for the Gender Equality Party, which was created in the wake of the 2029 Jina Revolution.*] Everyday people keep getting caught between political factions. There needs to be some sort of reckoning, and soon.

★

Nineteen Days until the Blaze

Roshan and I hit the road two mornings later. They drove the car; for me to do so was a safety hazard. When they'd first arrived in Abadan over a year and a half ago, they'd ogled the gasoline-fueled vehicles so many of us still used. In the United States, they said, electric cars were the norm, so they'd never seen the old gas cars.

'I'll let you know when we get access to such luxuries,' I'd told them dryly.

Despite the hour, sweat collected around my collar, under my arms. The temperatures around Iran had soared in the past decades, and Khuzestan was no stranger to these untenable heat waves. We were already past the deepest summer scorchers, but Mordad would offer us no reprieve.

The swampy ground squealed under the tyres when we moved from broken concrete to muddy road, skidding when we hit desiccated dirt sooner than expected. 'So are you going to tell me why we planned this excursion today?' Roshan asked, one hand slung on the wheel, the other tapping a rhythm against the car frame. 'Surely you're not hoping to catch one of the races.'

We didn't host the desert races as often as in other parts of Khuzestan, not when Abadan had been plagued with floods instead of droughts. I'd attended the races before, though: cars decked in metal grills and unwarranted chimneys and, on one that I'd seen, a gigantic metal claw. The fools even wore ridiculous grate-like masks on their faces, or corrugated sheets curled into horns, or – like they were an Indian bride – drooping gold chains.

Only an Iranian would flaunt gold while racing a tricked-out gas guzzler in the desert.

'I received news yesterday that those Tehrani kun goshadha are reneging on our agreement. They plan to retool *every* refinery for uranium instead of building a new one. With the plant and a new field so close by, and the waste dump sites outside of Haftgel, it becomes an easily maintainable loop.'

Roshan's brow furrowed. Ah, those Iranian eyebrows, or rather, eyebrow, the thick strands arching together like elegant bird wings. 'You told the Majles the discovery would lead to more money for us.'

'I didn't learn the news until after the meeting.' I sighed. 'And even if I had, I wouldn't have told those children. It would cause panic among them.'

Although most of our province's funds came from my coffers, I'd been called khasis for years, a stinginess inherent to prizing the people in my county above others. The insult rolled off me, but I was admittedly now concerned about what the others would do upon learning the news. Panic, yes – they couldn't take care of their own people without our money. Would they demand a new regional leader? The idea was laughable – I didn't doubt my people's loyalties – but I also knew that there were likely spies in my own camp, just as I had spies in theirs.

'That's a major problem, khaleh.' Roshan chanced a glance at me before attending to the empty road. 'It's bad enough that the poor have to use oil to begin with. What happens once there's no more available?'

I adjusted my cloth mask, protection against the dust whipping up around us in our doorless vehicle. 'That's precisely my concern, khaleh-jan.'

Abadan's refineries were the last ones left in Iran. Those in and around Kermanshah, Tehran, Esfahan, Bushehr, Mazarki – gone. The war with Iraq decades ago had destroyed many of our oil infrastructures; the pandemic and first Israeli War of Genocidal Aggression in the twenties prevented further expansion; and the tensions that boiled into the second Israeli War wiped out the rest that hadn't been decommissioned – aside from mine. Only China's interest had kept Abadan afloat, and what China wanted,

Iran acquiesced to, which meant I stayed in business.

We'd have gotten by on the other oil fields, but the loss of the refinery would decimate us. No oil for me and mine, and no oil money.

What I didn't understand – and needed to, fast – was why the government would lose out on the money I gave them to keep my operations running. It was no small amount, and the business it brought in from the Chinese was lucrative. They'd give that up for uranium? Why?

Shadegan's oil field – and impending uranium mine – was an hour outside Abadan city limits. We'd driven through what had once been a national park and was now a wasteland. When we'd redrawn the lines of the provinces many years past, I'd been sure to snag as many of the nearby oil fields as I could; easier than coordinating with my fellow Majles members.

We were reaching the outer edges of the field when a growing cloud of dust announced four vehicles racing towards us. Varying ridiculous accessories adorned each vehicle, from a mountain of spikes to an oil tankard with turrets to metal wings flaring with rusted paint. The peacocking of youth.

We rumbled to a stop, dust kicking up, the engine idling, as cars barrelled around us. I was a short woman, but no one had crossed me without feeling dire consequences; my reputation would have to extend to hooligans in the desert. They made no effort to hide their guns: slung over shoulders, resting casually on laps. I lifted myself so I was standing through the sunroof, palming my own pistol. I'd learned to be a decent shot despite the lack of an eye, but that would have been in a fair fight. Our car's customisations helped; I lifted the flaps that nocked my gun in place, decorative golden tassels flapping, and zeroed in on heat signatures.

Roshan shifted, a rifle appearing from under a layer of cloth. If I could have taken my attention off our visitors and looked at them in surprise, I would have. When had they gotten *that*?

'State your business,' shouted someone over the rumble of engines, revved to emphasise their words, when the cars finally slowed.

Ey, nadan! Did they not know the fuel for their vehicles came from my good graces?

'I will not tolerate such disrespect in *my* territory,' I snapped. 'State *your* business.'

Someone leaned over to whisper in the speaker's ear, whose attention shifted first to the gun-wielding lion-and-sun emblem on the car, then to me. 'So, you're the Oil Satrap of Abadan.'

Whenever I left my city, I made sure to wear a rusari of such flamboyant colours that it worked as my visual identifier. 'I see my reputation precedes me.' I loosened a dagger from inside my wrist and used it to pick nonexistent food from my teeth. 'And what can I do for you youngsters?'

The speaker, presumably the leader of this merry gang, wore a scarf around their face and neck like a rusari of their own. Across the mouth was a slab of white, like teeth in a skull, but rather than making them look menacing, they looked childish.

I wasn't worried, despite us being outnumbered. I was a damn good negotiator, and I had guards but minutes on our tail.

Below me, Roshan startled, then laughed. 'Ey, Jamshid-shah! Is that any way to treat my khaleh, pedar-sukhteh?'

Across from us, the leader made a sharp gesture, and each driver cut their engines. 'Roshan-jun,' they crooned as they hopped onto the sand, unwinding their scarf, 'is that you, aziz?'

'As God is my witness!' Roshan leapt from the car, and the two embraced.

What in God's good name...

'Khaleh, come meet Jamshid Alizadeh,' Roshan called. 'Pofak sar is a friend of mine.'

When Roshan had first moved to Iran, I'd encouraged

them to make friends. We had groups in Abadan to facilitate such relationships, and they'd joined me at enough Majles meetings to meet those who accompanied the other leaders. This Jamshid was a stranger, though, and that disturbed me.

The youth clasped a hand to their breast and bowed in my direction. While I was not in the business of assuming gender, from a distance, I could not place their youth's slight frame, their wrapped bald head. Upon closer inspection, though, I understood the visual markers I'd confused. The youth's chest had been bound, and the hairs on their lips and cheek were the fine markers of one who'd long waxed until they'd stopped. Born after the government no longer subsidised gender-affirming care, I'd wager. A pity that the one good thing those Islamist pigs gave those of my ilk had been dismantled after the revolution.

'My apologies for being rude, khaleh,' said this Jamshid. 'I patrol this area for possible thieves.'

'Under whose orders?' I asked, keeping my voice pleasant.

'The Khuzestan Majles, of course.'

Kiram tu dahanesh, I doubted that. More likely, one of the other leaders was trying to gain a foothold in my jurisdiction without starting a war.

'So what's the latest, aziz?' Roshan gestured to the road ahead of us. 'We were going to check on the fields, see the progress on the mine.'

'It's supposed to be glorious,' said Jamshid, 'though not sure who that glory is for. Definitely not us.' They nodded to our gas vehicles. 'The operations look much the same from out here, anyway. But I'm afraid I can't share more than that.'

I was going to kick Ahvazi's ass when I saw them next. When had they become bold enough to try and undermine me like this? It had to be them; theirs was the county neighbouring mine.

Roshan laughed. 'We should blow it up. Start over fresh, with energy for all. Surely the collateral damage alone would get others to sit up and pay attention, maybe even the international community. Kickstart another revolution.'

Cheers erupted from the gang, ululations reverberating in the empty air, at least one snapping beshkan piercing the heat.

Calling myself a good woman would be a lie. Caring for the people of Abadan meant I made decisions that left victims in its wake. I was aware I doomed people to die when I withheld aid so that my families could eat. When Shushtari and Izehi and the others brought reports of their desperate need, and I refused them, I knew their blood was on my hands. Still, I prayed. Still, I wished peace upon my brethren. But I was no fool: My death would be a reckoning, and the Day of Judgment would not view me kindly.

Even so, the suggestion Roshan made, and the resulting enthusiasm from the others, chilled me. When had my nibling become so ruthless? Was it a joke to save face in front of this friend? My eye itched, desperate for relubrication.

I needed information, and there were easy ways of making people talk. From my back pocket, I slid out a fraction of the cash I carried with me. Deliberately, I began to count out bills, paying attention to when Jamshid's eyes began to widen.

'Tell me, Jamshid-jan.' I slid the bills out and offered them. 'This uranium deposit. Surely it makes no sense for the government to hinder us while mining their little operation.'

'Oh, this deposit is bigger than the other ones combined,' said Jamshid cheerfully, pocketing the cash. 'And those geologists are pretty sure there are overlaps in other fields too, more than what the country can use. But you didn't hear that from me.'

More than what the country can use. More than what the rich could use. But not more than what other countries might pay handsomely for.

Shit.

*

Excerpted Letter from Nasrin Etezadi
dated 24 Azar 1492 / 15 December 2050

[…] Despite all I've written above, I find myself at a loss to write the truth of what I need, before it's too late. I beg you, my dearest sister, to watch over Roshan.

How I fear for my child and their future. Not a child, they'd remind me, and I'd try so hard not to laugh at their annoyance; no, not a child, but my child, and soon I will be gone and unable to guide them. How often I tell them how their father's own struggles took him from us, that his pregnancy and the clinical trials around our two-egg embryo exacerbated what had already bubbled to the surface, but no genetic argument can convince Roshan their pain may be unique to them but not to the world, that we have medicine to help them weather their internal storms. But for as much as they're my child, they are an adult, and I cannot force them to seek help.

So please, my sister. Please save Roshan from themself before we both lose them.

*

Thirteen Days until the Blaze

I parked the motorboat by the shore, looping the rope over a rotting post. Roshan shaded their eyes and craned their neck up, staring at the ripening dates – maybe a week or two before most of the harvest was ready, but the ground was already littered with half-consumed, half-rotting offerings, remnants of whatever life remained.

This area used to be covered in palms, but our water had long grown too salty. How sad they looked, dried husks drooping over sodden ground. Rotten logs abandoned to their lichenous fate. That there were any trees left felt like a miracle, God be praised.

We'd buried my sister's ashes here, carried in a small wooden box; any samples of Pedar-jan's khatam kari had been lost, I'd thought, until Roshan had stepped off that plane with it in hand. I'd been surprised to hear she'd been cremated, but my sister never did care for religious traditions. I'd spent the last several decades of my life reconnecting with our faith, while she'd spent hers denying it.

We used to sneak off here, in the days when our hunger could not be soothed. In the days when we knew two little girls could slip through the cracks. Perhaps it was good that she'd gotten out of Iran. For so many years – too many, perhaps – I'd been angry with her decision to leave; instead of fighting to save our country, she'd left it for our brethren to piece together. For *me* to piece together.

My mind turned, as it so often did these months, to the final letter my sister had sent along with her child and ashes, written mere weeks before her death. Roshan's mental health struggles were known to me – how many times Nasrin had called, her voice thick with tears, bemoaning the choices Roshan had made, the ways they'd harmed themself. How often I'd told her they could not be helped unless they were willing to help themself. But I had not appreciated the extent to which they, like their late father before them, were struggling. And that letter reminded me again that we were not dealing with a child, but someone who would not thank us should their autonomy be taken from them.

'Khaleh-jun,' my nibling said now, as we left the muddy bank for abandoned trees further in and the little sign we'd left as a grave marker. 'I was wondering…'

We knelt at the site where we'd buried my sister's ashes over eighteen months before. I pressed my fingers into the earth, murmuring a prayer for the dead. I may have been a shit Muslim, but I could recite my surahs when needed.

Roshan squatted beside me, staring blankly at the spot where my fingers met dirt. They wiped their cheeks on their sleeve, thin fabric drawing down their arms. 'I miss her.'

'Me too, asalam,' I murmured. 'Abji would have done

anything to be with us.' We stared for another beat at where we'd buried that wooden box. 'So, you were wondering?'

Roshan's breaths laboured. They swallowed, audible in the thick silence. At least the humidity was at bay until the winter months.

'The shift to uranium will disrupt your operations,' they said at last. 'Which means you're going to have to figure out a new way to take care of your county, and a new source of income to send over for the rest of them. Can't you, I don't know, sabotage the government's plans? Stop them from mining – physically? At least, until you have a new plan.'

Business is business, I always said, but the key part was what followed: *as God wills it.* I liked pretty things as much as the next Iranian, but at the cost of children's swollen bellies and sunken eyes?

'That might work for a while, and I have considered it,' I admitted. 'But it puts people in danger at a time when we're holding our breath to see what happens next. The "Morality Party", or whatever the hell the old Islamists are calling themselves, was biding its time as the Pahlavis fought internally for office. Look at how much of the country has become uninhabitable as they hemmed and hawed over this sustainability switch. Every date palm orchard in Abadan has gone to shit. Our neighbour Mahtab, one of your mother's best friends – her son is part of the crew operating the underground pipe network to make ends meet, despite the dangers. Bagherzadeh's election last year was no coincidence.'

One might think, given another revolution the moment his mentor died, our Khamenei-trained president and the other Twelvers would take the hint. But my sister wouldn't have thought so – she'd have pointed out that this is what religion does, offering empty hope during difficult times. I went to masjid every Friday and tried to be a good Muslim – banditry notwithstanding – but our country's fraught history proved her right.

'That's the problem,' Roshan said. 'We need leadership willing to think outside of what we've always done. Please don't take this as criticism of you – I'm thinking on a larger level, a national level. And I want to help make change, khaleh, even when the costs are high. But Lotfi-agha said–'

It took me a moment to place who Roshan was talking about. The habit of referring to other Majles members by our regions of control started some ten-odd years back, when Izeh was going through such upheavals that every meeting for six months saw a new leader. I hadn't heard Shushtari's given name in years.

'Akh, martikeh,' I muttered. 'When did you two grow so close?'

Roshan hesitated. 'Don't be mad, khaleh. He's been kind to me.'

I sighed. 'I'm not mad, azizam. But I'd be wary of Shushtari's motives. Ahvazi and I are the ones directly impacted by the uranium mining. His stake in this is only as it pertains to the funds he'll receive.' And I knew he had his hands in other pockets. Had Shushtar County been on my borders, I would have wondered if that so-called patrol with Roshan's new friends had been at his behest.

When Roshan didn't respond, I said, 'What did he tell you?'

'Well...' Roshan dragged their finger through the sandy soil. 'He said it would be tricky for Iranians to accept me in any leadership position.'

My knees, no longer as spry as they once were, protested my continual crouch. I eased myself up, grunting at the effort. 'And why would he say that?'

They didn't look at me as their sand sketch turned into loops and swirls. 'He said they'll never accept me as one of them. As Iranian.'

I scoffed. 'You are Iranian.'

'But I'm American, too,' they said. 'I never liked calling

myself that, and it's not like the white kids ever saw me as one of them. But I am. Or, at least' – the words poured out of them faster – 'I'm too American for the Iranians, like I'm too Iranian for the Americans. Like I'm never enough or far too much. Like no one can place what I am or where I belong. I thought it was bad enough that I'm not a man or woman, but then throw this onto the mix, and it feels like no one knows what to do with me.'

I wanted to keep my people fed, yes. But that was a responsibility, and here I burned on a personal level: I wanted to do right by a sister I'd loved so acutely, I'd internally narrated my life to her for three decades. Her little boghzaleh was no longer so little, no longer soft, and how I wished I could reach back to help them retain their innocence and hope.

Three suicide attempts between the ages of fourteen and twenty would destroy that in anyone.

I'd never wanted children of my own, even when my beloved Marzieh was alive. There was no shortage of orphans we could have adopted, and she'd wanted to, desperately – but the responsibility of children made my balls become one.

Roshan was different. Roshan was my *sister's* child. And my sister was gone, and they had no one else but me.

How could I have comforted them? How could I have assured them their worries were unfounded? The feeling of being both too much and too little. I did not think that was something so unique to a diasporic experience, but did I know what it was like to straddle so many cultures? Being Lur, and having Kurdish roots on my mother's side to boot, still made me Iranian. I never saw our country's various peoples as less than that.

I reached for a conversation I'd had with my right-hand woman years ago. 'Sohaila isn't Persian, you know,' I told them. 'She's an Arab Iranian.'

'Feels like a contradiction,' muttered Roshan.

I chuckled. 'Being so close to the border, many of us grew up watching Arab television and eating Arab foods. My point is, Sohaila has never doubted where she belonged, even as she also was of multiple places, like you. You are home, khaleh. You are one of us. Don't doubt it.'

Roshan turned away and didn't respond, as if I'd said the wrong thing.

★

Sampled decrypted messages
dated between 9 and 27 Mordad 1492

Blueprints received and distributed. Awaiting further instructions.
-R

Retrieved materials. Hidden in Khorramshahr cache.
-J

Recruits confirmed, will arrive 23 Mordad. R, distribute green patches upon arrival.
-S

Patches distributed. Positioning confirmed.
-R

Oil Satrap suspicious? Unhappy about stop.
-J

No. Still think we should consider bringing her in.
-R

At all costs, do not alert Abadani.
-S

★

Zero Hours Until the Blaze
28 Mordad 1492 / 18 August 2053

The explosion shook us in the middle of the meeting.

I was on my feet, pistol in hand, before the others could react. The rest of the Khuzestan Majles had arrived earlier in the week to herd their people as protests had begun in my streets. NO NUCLEAR FOR THE RICH UNTIL NUCLEAR FOR THE POOR was the major rallying point, useless though it seemed.

Pounding rattled the door. Unfortunately, it only swung inward, so I couldn't kick it, instead opting to have my pistol raised when I wrenched it open. Sohaila's wide-eyed face greeted me.

'The refineries,' she breathed.

I swore, holstered my gun, and took off after her as the others called out in confusion. We, of course, had guards crawling everywhere in the refineries, especially now that the officials had come to tour them for prospective changes.

Ahvazi bolted through the door before it could shut behind me, hot on my heels, determination on their face. Before we swung down the stairs, I chanced a look back. The other Majles members milled about, looking troubled, except for Shushtari. He stared directly at me, face unreadable.

I didn't have time for him.

Another explosion shook our building. Ahvazi's long strides overtook mine, and they reached the outer door first, holding it open just long enough for me and Sohaila to get through. An earthquake? A cyclone?

We hopped into the doorless vehicle parked haphazardly in front of our meeting building, and Sohaila gassed it. Ahvazi started talking into a headset, agitated taps only ending when they turned to me. 'We need to control the narrative before it spins out of control. The media is already having a frenzy.'

They were absolutely right. Anxiety gripped my belly as I projected calm. 'The protestors?'

'Scattered with the initial blasts.'

'And... the officials?'

Ahvazi's grim silence answered that question. 'Did you order this?' they accused, eyes narrowing.

'I'm not a fool,' I snapped.

With Sohaila's driving, we raced past parked gas-based vehicles that were supposedly retired a decade ago and people who came out of their homes to see what the commotion was about before we arrivied at a wall of reporters and civilians, with guards barring them from moving through.

I could smell it before we'd arrived, the smoke. With water as scarce as it was, fire departments around the country had taken to using sand to smother all-too-common flames, but there wasn't enough nearby to tame this inferno – they'd have to fly it in. How could buildings made of metal lead to such destruction?

Well... buildings containing crude and refined oil. The smell of gasoline was strong enough to make me sick.

We waded through the throng, our people on duty allowing us to slip past. Heat blew against my face like summer's kiss. Ahvazi pressed fingers to their headset and swore so profusely, I would have given them a mocking *deh!* in another context. 'Khak tu sareshun, they've hit the roads out of the city.' They began to bark orders to their own people as I sent Sohaila on a scouting mission and hoisted myself against a statue to peer around.

Where was my nibling? Why hadn't the other council members mobilised their forces? *How had this happened?*

When Roshan had made their foolhardy joke weeks ago to their friend in the desert, I thought they'd meant destroying the mine. But no – they meant the latest building facilities, the ones that would link the various refineries in Abadan into one giant complex. The facilities some of the most powerful governmental officials had been touring.

But it couldn't be them – how could it be them? How many hundreds, if not thousands, of Abadan's people would be caught in the fallout? Innocents were employed in the refinery. Our entire province depended on them. Such damage would–

A helicopter veered towards us as others tried to contain the blaze. I watched as so much of my life's work went up in smoke, with my people trapped inside.

★

BREAKING NEWS
TOP IRANIAN OFFICIALS CAUGHT IN DEADLY
REFINERY FIRE

Abadan, Iran – Officials touring the historic oil refineries in the southwestern city of Abadan were caught inside a deadly blaze.

With the conclusion of the fifth and final planned nuclear energy summit in Tehran, officials moved south to the projected site of a new uranium refinery complex in Abadan, a conversion of the historic oil refineries that were among the last ones decommissioned in 2041. With Abadan's proximity to the nuclear plant in Darkhoveyn (under 50 kilometres) and the uranium deposit in what was once the Shadegan oil fields (under 70 kilometres), Abadan's converted refineries were slated to contribute 1.2 trillion rials to the Iranian economy.

Demonstrations against the reversion of the refinery from oil to nuclear began earlier in the week. 'Sure, people in Tehran have their nuclear energy,' said one of the protestors, who wished to remain anonymous. 'But when we're living in rural communities, we don't have access to anything but gasoline. And when the government has forsaken these areas as unlivable, those of us forced to remain are left stranded.'

Protests remained peaceful until the third day of the tour,

when explosions hit the proposed uranium refinery sites, roads leading out of Abadan, and the partially constructed uranium mine in Shadegan. Officials say use of illegal oil and gasoline, explosives, and a knowledge of the refinery layouts point to the perpetrators having internal assistance in pulling off this attack.

A small group of individuals have come forth claiming responsibility for the action via a viral video. In it, a tall, masked individual stands in the centre of a pyre and declares their intent to eject the 'old guard' from government and give the country a chance at fresh voices in power.

'As long as Iranians are under the yoke of the past,' says the masked individual, 'there will never be true progress. I send this as a message to Iranians around the world: We must support our brethren as they fight for access to basic necessities, let alone the promises of the '29 Revolution. Long has self-immolation been a tool for Iranians to speak out against government injustices. My hope is that my death today, and the deaths of those in this building, will lead to real, lasting change in Iran.'

While the name of the speaker is not yet known, anonymous sources point to an Iranian born in the United States, prompting speculation about that government's involvement. The US Embassy has denied the accusations.

But for some, the vision of the flames provoked a different reaction.

'The burning of a cinema in Abadan stoked the flames of the 1979 Revolution,' said one protestor. 'That tragedy was the beginning of the end for the monarchy. Perhaps this one will wake up the government and make them realise they can't ignore the poor to satisfy the rich.'

Glossary

Abji: a term of endearment for one's (usually older) sister.

Agha: 'mister'; can be used as a suffix, prefix, or on its own.

Akh: a guttural sound with a meaning similar to 'tsk'.

Asalam: literally, 'my honey'; a term of endearment.

Ayatollah: high-ranking clergy of Twelver Shia Islam.

Aziz: 'dear one'; a term of endearment.

Azizam: 'my dear'.

Azizan: 'dear ones,' plural of 'aziz'.

Beshkan: a snap where the index finger of one hand is dragged across the index finger (particularly knuckle) of the other.

Bi gheirat: literally, 'without honor'; an insult on someone's morals or a judgement on someone's actions.

Boghzaleh: a goat's child ('kid').

Deh: a sound indicating shock.

Ey: an apostrophe, exclamatory figure of speech.

Goh tu dahanet: literally, 'shit in your mouth'; an insult.

-jan: literally, 'life'; used as a suffix or on its own as a term of endearment.

-jun: the colloquial pronunciation of 'jan'.

Kiram tu dahanesh: literally, 'my dick in their mouth'; a variation on 'kiram tu dahanet', an insulting phrase.

Khak tu sareshun: literally, 'dirt on their heads'; depending on tone and context, comparable to 'shame on them' or 'fuck them'.

Khasis: stingy; considered a negative personality trait.

Khaleh: maternal aunt.

Khatam kari: a traditional art form where geometrical patterns are inlaid into a surface

Kos kholha: literally, 'idiot pussies'; a pluralised version of '*kos khol*,' an insult on one's intelligence.

Kun goshadha: literally, 'those with long butts'; a plural version of 'kun goshad', an insult for laziness.

Lur: an Iranian ethnic group with multiple linguistic dialects.

Madar-jendeh: literally, 'one whose mother is a whore'; comparable to 'motherfucker'.

Majles: a term for a gathering or council; used also for the governmental parliament.

Martikeh: a belittling insult to a man.

Masjid: mosque.

Mordad: a month corresponding roughly to August in the Gregorian calendar.

Morde shur: literally, 'one who washes the dead'; an insult.

Nadan: literally, 'one who does not know'; an insult for foolishness.

Pedar-jan: literally, 'dear father'; often used for grandfathers.

Pedar-sagha: literally, 'father of dogs'; a pluralised version of '*pedar-sag,*' an insult.

Pedar-sukhteh: literally, 'burnt father' or 'one whose father is burnt'; often used for someone who causes mischief or is a troublemaker; can be used affectionately.

Pofak sar: literally, '[cheese] puff head'; an insult to mean empty-headed; often used teasingly.

Rusari: literally, 'that which is worn on your head'; a headscarf often used as a hijab.

Shah: literally, 'king'; can be used as a suffix, prefix, or on its own. Used in reference to King. Jamshid, legendary ruler from the Persian *Book of Kings*.

Surah: A chapter in the Quran.

Ya Ali madad: literally, 'O Ali, assistance'; an invocation to the exalted aspect of God via one of the 99 Names for the love of the Prophet Mohammad's son-in-law Ali; often used to ask for strength.

The Tomb

Fereshteh Ahmadi

Translated by Sholeh Wolpé

IF YOU CAN ENDURE a three-hour drive from Semnan to the only access road to the northeast of Tehran, then cross the Hesarak Station suspension bridge, hike up a winding path until you reach Eysh Heights and look up at the balcony of my grandmother Mina's house, in that moment, you'd think you are inside a painting by Jacek Yerka, that crazy artist from Poland.

I'm standing in front of Mina's house with my back to the Pit, facing the crown of the hill. It's as if I'm a grey, deformed dot in one of that Polish artist's paintings, standing in front of an explosion of brilliant pigments. I don't dare turn my head around and look at what's behind me. One must simply stare directly ahead, careful not to let the eyes wander right or left, or else thick black ink will spread itself in one's field of vision and transform the glorious, brilliant colours of the house and everything behind it – those vibrant blocks stretching all the way to the top of the mountain – into something terrifyingly ugly. Yerka's paintings are like that; you mustn't let the comfy armchair or the rainbow inside the frame mislead you because just a little yonder is a sheer cliff, waiting for you.

Mina would have never stayed here had she not been a bit cuckoo. She's totally nuts. She's been this way since she was a teenager. Personally, I don't have a problem with loonies, but my mother and the rest have abandoned her because of her crazy antics.

I'm about to enter the building to slip off my overalls when I spot Carla standing on the second-floor balcony, hands on her waist, looking down at me. She is wearing a sleeveless orange top and a long, loose turquoise skirt. 'How are you, kid?' she says softly in her funny accent. 'Coming up?'

I wave and mime: *Not now*. Her clingy top shows off her smooth, flat chest as if she has never had breasts. Mina says Carla didn't have cancer. 'She just got rid of them. Lots of women do. To straighten their backs and feel comfortable, light on their feet. Besides, what would they want breasts for anyway?'

Mina knows I'm well acquainted with Carla's body, but she still insists on telling me about it with loads of mockery and sarcasm. She does it because she thinks it will loosen my tongue. The first time I saw those parallel, sinuous lines on Carla's white, skinny body, I simply rode my fingers over them, not in a way that might give the impression I was repulsed but in a nonchalant manner as if I were caressing her waist or her stomach; or as if I were a Martian and all women on Mars looked exactly the way she did. Totally normal. I knew that if I exhaled funny, or let my eyes linger even for a moment on those lines, she would no longer want me. But as it happens, she does still want me. She leans over the railings and watches me go inside. I discard my overalls in Mina's storage room. She doesn't let anyone into her home in what she calls 'filthy attire'. Before I go upstairs, I stop and finally allow myself to turn around and look at the Pit.

They have flocked here from every corner of the world: breastless women, genderless movements, environmentalists, scientists, photographers, wandering artists, fearless journalists, runaway lovers, nudists, treasure hunters, explorers of new ideas, followers of new religions more respectful of nature's fury, and adventurers. They've come because they find the Pit a source of great inspiration. Most arrived on the heels of the fleeing residents of Tehran, a sinking city they renamed *Godal*, the Pit. Mina has never set foot outside of the Pit. She says she doesn't want to see the stinking lake where we now live or any of the so-called new capitals. Mina still calls it Tehran, which annoys my mother no end. Over the phone, Mina intentionally repeats the word to needle her because it's been three or four years since her daughter's last visit.

They built that lake where my mother now lives by taking water from the Caspian Sea so as to develop the deserts around Semnan, Garmsar, Shahroud and Qom. After that, everything and everyone relocated: people, water, animals, even the capital itself. Soon, a handful of new animals showed up. Then, transparent mosquitoes started flying a metre above the lake, giving it the illusion of a whirling kaleidoscope of colours. That, in turn, became a tourist attraction which generated income for the new capital and so, no one made a fuss over the leafless, barren trees on whose trunks the mosquitoes lay their eggs, slathering it with yellow slime, a parasitic environment that fed thousands of larvae. In Qom and Semnan, the increased humidity affected the development of the desert's tiny, timid reptiles: instead of shedding their skin, they began to grow more layers and grew bigger. They weren't yet large enough to create any kind of panic, but a group of dinosaur enthusiasts started monitoring these changes with excitement. They believed dinosaurs would one day return and reclaim their land. The group even began to identify and categorise the reptiles' various species. They invited me to join their project because of my perspective on history. I respectfully accepted their invitation even though I knew I could be of no help. I was just an employee of the Department of Reconstruction of History whose job it was to collect credentials, titles and documents. Still, by joining their group I gave the impression that I could be of some use.

When I travel to Tehran for business, I often stop by to see Mina. I am the only non-virtual link between her and the rest of the family. She calls me her 'offline grandchild'.

Upstairs, the front light of Mina's apartment is on. When I step onto the landing, the door flings open. It's impossible to surprise my grandmother. She always knows. Always knows everything. For instance, I hadn't told her I was coming. I wanted to mess with her, the way she always messes with me. Every time she messages me, she goes on and on about some new event in Tehran to pique my interest and drag me here, but I know better. I analyse her cunning words to figure out what she's really after. She always pretends she is inviting me simply because she loves my company or is interested in what I like and do, and that she doesn't need anything from me and is quite able to work everything out for herself. So, I leave her in suspense and never say when or if I'm coming. Still, more often than not, she wins the game by pretending she doesn't care. This time, however, it's different. She sent me message after message to hurry over because time was running out. She was restless and something strange was going on in her head. She even started her message with: 'My dear Saman', which made me laugh. From what I could gather from her tangled messages, she was alarmed by the latest land collapse in a street behind Sae'i Park. It had stirred up quite a controversy. The old Clock Museum had sunk into the ground and now other things were being uncovered, literally. These new revelations have revived the old story of the long-forgotten Coup, which has sent Mina into a state of frenzy. In one of her messages, she wrote: 'The earth has given us back our old stories.'

I forgot to smoke my cigarette downstairs to avoid having to light up on Mina's balcony facing that view. Mina always sits and smokes out there, looking at it! She lounges and puffs away! I could never figure out how she stands it. Doesn't the sadness crush her heart? My mother and others begged Mina to give up living on this mountain and join the rest of the family. At first, I thought they didn't visit her in Tehran because they were afraid of getting sick or becoming short of breath. But when, for the first time, I took in Tehran from Mina's balcony, I felt my heart muscles tighten. That's when I understood why Mina's children and grandchildren didn't want to come here, no matter what. The black hole that breathes under Mina's feet puffs its hot breath into your face and sucks out all joy and laughter from your soul. Its moan echoes between the walls of your skull without any respite or possibility of escape until it finally settles into the depths of your being.

The first ones to flee were the crows. At the time, Mina had said, 'Don't mind their unchiselled bodies or their awful caw-caws. They are very dear. Dear, smart, and ancient. Have you ever seen the skeleton of a dead crow? Exactly! That's how they are. At the first sign of calamity, they just pack up and leave.' The smart residents of Tehran followed the crows and left as well; the rest joined in later waves of migration. Some departed after gas pipes exploded, others left after rumours began to circulate that little people were popping out of the ground like grasshoppers or moths. Mina, however, didn't even join the last wave of emigrants three years ago when the government announced the closure of all medical and health facilities – everything but select emergency service locations for those with residence cards. Water supply and electricity services were limited to specific service areas as well. At the time, Mina had just finished furnishing her house as if she were a new bride. She had made a fortress of it on this mountain where life still goes on, though not to everyone's taste. Like I said: breastless women, genderless movements, environmentalists, scientists, photographers, wandering artists, fearless journalists and the rest.

Station Number 1, the highest stop on the cable car route, is concealed from view by the colourful apartments that climb the side of the mountain. Station Number 5 offers easy access to the Pit and is only a few steps away from Mina's house. Even though the air up here is generally clear enough to breathe, the station is hazy and glum, and the guardroom is enveloped in a grey halo. This is probably because it is directly linked to the Pit by the cable car. The station attendant is an old hunchback who smokes like a chimney and doesn't talk to anyone. They say the stench of the Pit has made its inhabitants addicted to it. Mina must also be addicted because she seems unbothered by the things she sees. For the residents of the new capital, even hearing the news about the Pit is unsettling. Most of them prefer to cut and throw away that part of their past. The government supports this collective amnesia and has omitted photos of the old Tehran from school textbooks. In the chapter on Iran's ancient capitals, Tehran receives only a passing reference.

But we, in the Historiography and Document Preservation Committee, under the supervision of famous Iranologist Edward Tyson, continue our work regardless of the government's politics and policies. Thanks to Tyson's influence, we have no problem collecting and preserving documents, but in content production and data analysis, we have our differences and endless disputes. Once I took home a copy of an old photo of Tajrish Square[1] and its surrounding markets. When I showed it to my mother, she pushed my hand away as if I were showing her a picture of a mutilated corpse. Each time I return home from Tehran, she avoids getting too close, saying, 'You've brought home the stench of that place.' She doesn't ask about Mina, as if she knows everything there is to know about her and that it's no big deal she's abandoned her 84-year-old mother in Tehran. Most people in our family talk about Mina as if she's in a mental asylum or her madness is contagious and that's the reason no one goes to see her, except me, of course, who they regard as a bit of a lunatic as well. But even before all this, none of them trusted Mina. They spread gossip and rumours about her mental state. Everyone was convinced that she suffered from melancholia and that she lived in cloud cuckoo land without the aid of drugs.

When Tehran began to disappear, Mina too began to distance herself from everyone. As the city sank 36 centimetres a year, Mina moved the equivalent distance away from the rest of us. At first, no one talked about the sinkings but then the municipal authorities began to warn against high-risk locations: places with clay soils, points located on fault lines or above the routes of Tehran's old qanats,[2] places where excessive extraction of underground water continued... But they didn't even dare publish these maps which, for some unknown reason, were marked as second editions. People watched and prayed and didn't believe that Tehran would finally drop like a wounded soldier on its knees and fall apart. It was not difficult to guess where things were heading and how it would all end, but no one wanted to believe the city's inevitable fate – except crazy Mina.

The old woman's pale eyes could see into the distance, and now it was as if she was looking into the future. 'Tehran isn't dead yet,' she says. 'This mountain's rivers may be frail and seasonal but they still drip like serum into that old soldier's body and keep it alive.' At this, she recites a verse from the Quran: 'And we appointed mountains as the nails of the earth.'

Twenty years ago, when nobody was paying attention to the news, Mina started buying up land on this mountain. By the time my mother realised she couldn't stop her, she called a family meeting. They reviewed all the crazy things the old woman had been doing and looked for some legal means to block her from her own bank account. My aunt's husband found a savvy lawyer who gathered enough testimonies to obtain a certificate pronouncing the old woman delusional and mentally incompetent. Mina lost access to her account and had to stop buying plots of land. Instead, she poured her energy into the single piece of land the deed to which she had been able to hide and keep, and on which she subsequently built this house.

The whole story has two sides, of course, two perspectives. But the long and the short of it is that the Azad University, in those years, was spread out in the northwest mountains of Tehran. At some point, they began selling plots of land on this high, rocky mountain. They offered them to their faculty and retired employees at a cheap price with low-interest loans. Shortly after, a dispute between the Department of Natural Resources and the university led to a ban on the construction of homes above 1800 metres. The pensioners and faculty members who had bought the plots panicked and tried to get their money back from the university. Mina bought her friend's land and tried to buy two or three more. There was a frenzy among the landowners to obtain Mina's phone number to unload their bad investments. That's when my mother and the rest of the family stepped in. Mina hid the deed to the original plot of land she had managed to buy and, later, when the municipality passed a new law allowing construction at higher points, her land skyrocketed in value. But now she had lost access to her money, so she partnered with Neil and Carla, a couple who, like the other foreigners, had come to the Pit in search of adventure, to build a multi-unit apartment building. They gave Mina two units and kept the rest for themselves. In the meantime, Tehran kept its shoulder to the wheel and spread itself up the mountain, bit by bit, higher and higher.

I was old enough in those days to remember what it was like. The subways had stopped running because the tunnels were in constant danger of collapse. One of the East-West lines was so badly damaged, it was as if a giant had crushed it under its feet. We had been among the smart ones to establish ourselves in the new capital long before all this destruction came to pass. Baba, who used to bribe a guy to obtain unannounced information, had managed to buy a lot of cheap land in Semnan and Shahrood. That's how we were able to quickly pick up our tails and escape Tehran. Shortly after our move, administrative and commercial centres were relocated to Garmsar and recreational facilities were divided between Semnan, Qom and Shahrood. Everyone left Tehran except those who were trapped here by their work commitments or simply because they had nowhere else to go. Tehran became an ailing patient whose fever Mina wanted to monitor from her home up on the mountain. As the city exuded a foul vapour from its open pores, Mina would murmur: 'And we appointed the mountains as the nails of the earth.' It was as if Tehran had put its head on Mina's lap and she was rocking it from side to side like an old southern woman, caressing its head and singing it mournful songs.

I throw a pebble at the balcony from the first floor landing. Then another at the window. I'm about to throw a third when the balcony door opens and the small figure of an old woman ambles towards the railing. Her thin, grey hair is spiked up, creating a white halo around her head. She doesn't see as well as she used to but her hearing more than compensates for that. She stares right at me but isn't quite sure if it's me. I raise my voice and say: 'Mina, Mina come down. I haven't got long, I have to get back before dark. Come down.' Sometimes I like to play bossy, but she usually ignores me, which is like throwing hot water on ice. She buzzes the iron door open obliging me to go up. The ground floor is Carla and Neil's studio and laboratory. Mina is friendly towards the couple and sometimes invites them up for tea. Her true intention is, of course, to learn what they are up to. I'm sure she secretly visits their laboratory when they're not home but probably hasn't yet found anything remarkable enough to tattle about. Neil's work involves researching changes in the ecosystem and he is a member of ICAR's research team. But Mina is certain they're spies. The idea of foreigners as spies is a two- or three-hundred-year-old legacy that still afflicts our older generation.

The door of the laboratory is ajar. I peer in. Neil is sitting in dim light at his desk, scribbling on a large piece of paper. He looks up and I quickly pull away and run up the stairs. Mina has left the door open. I'm about to go in when I see Carla on top of the stairs. She whispers, 'Will you come see me too?' I whisper back: 'I don't know. Maybe next time.'

Once, when Neil was not home, Carla had asked me to come up and see her photos. But what she showed me weren't photographs at all. They were strange, high-contrast black and white collages of patterns with splashes of colour. That was the day I learned about Jacek Yerka's paintings.

Now, I anxiously glance down the stairs, then run a few steps up. Carla hurries down a few and we hug and kiss. I love pressing her flat chest against mine. She knows that and loves that I love it. I am aroused by the absence of her breasts. I give her a peck under the ear and run back downstairs. Mina is in the kitchen making a racket with plates and bowls. I throw myself on the large, prehistoric sofa. 'Mina Khanum, what are you up to now?' I say. 'You've got me here… at your service. I know you've been cracking nuts with your tail and have tricked me to come, but you don't have to invent a long tale each time to lure me here. Just say it straight that you miss me.'

Mina slams a cup of tea on the table in front of me. 'Shut it,' she says.

I open my bag and take out the provisions my mother has sent to assuage her guilty conscience: homemade sponge cakes, dried lemons and figs, sesame and flax seeds which she obsessively forces us to eat, and something wrapped in tissue paper. There are also several types of herbal medicines, their names scribbled on each jar, which my grandmother probably knows what to do with. Lately, eating that stuff is all the rage. *Bring nature back into your body,* the slogan reads.

Mina surveys it all with a frown, then says: 'As if you can't find any of this here. Tell your mother we have everything. People live here and get by just fine, as you can see.' She tears into the tissue paper, as she's saying this, and pulls out a mustard-coloured coat and skirt. The frown doesn't leave her face, but I know it's a pretence and that she likes the suit. I launch into a barrage of family news: from the birth of her latest great grandchild, to another's acceptance into a good university, to marriages and… but this time she isn't listening for real. She pulls up a photo on her tablet and shows it to me. It is an aerial photo of a site that recently sank into the ground. She pinches the photo open to reveal the surrounding streets. I laugh and say: 'I already knew what happened to that house. Saw it on the news a few days ago.'

She begins to scroll through other photos as if she's forgotten I'm here. She brings the illuminated tablet up to her face as if she is speaking to it. 'First, I found out a new pit has been found. Then I saw Clara put on her shawl and hat, pick up her big expensive camera and get ready to go out. I ask what the heck is she going to do out there. She says a fascinating old shelter has been found. They call everything "fascinating".'

'Shelter?' I ask.

'Exactly! That's what I said to her: Shelter? From the war? But then she was confused. Wanted to know which war I was talking about. So I told her. The Iraq-Iran War. The shelters are from that era. From the time of rockets. I was ten or twelve years old. You must've had them too, I told her, during war. At first, Clara seemed to listen with concern but then she suddenly hit her own forehead and said, "Oh that was dumb of me. No. Not a shelter. I meant to say a hiding place."'

Mina shakes her head and says: 'It drives a person up the wall trying to speak to this Carla. Anyway, she said a hiding place has been found and that it belonged to a man who's been missing since the 1979 revolution. Everyone thought he was either dead or living in exile somewhere under a fake name. Carla didn't remember his name but said he died about forty-five years ago and was buried in the same hiding place.'

Mina had insisted that Clara should find the man's name and Clara had made a few calls. His name was Massoud Keyvani and his hiding place was located on Vozara Street, right behind Sa'i Park on the back side of the Clock Museum, an old building that had remained intact from the second Pahlavi era.[3] At first, the building was used as a residence but then it was confiscated by the government and turned into a museum.

I chuckle because I'm way ahead of Mina on this. I know the ins and outs of this particular discovery. I wait for her to ask something so I can bombard her with information, but she just sips her tea in silence and stares at the aerial photo. Then she says: 'I was there. Inside that very building.'

Her eyes droop and she suddenly looks helpless and fragile. She taps the image with her thin, bony finger. 'I was here,' she says. 'In 1985. I was sixteen years old.'

'Why on earth were you there?' I ask.

'An influential family lived here,' she says. 'One of those with clout and history. How strange that the building was not confiscated right after the revolution. The back door opened to a set of stairs leading to the park. That's where I used to take my school books and do all my studying, not to mention get up to mischief – right there. I have to go see it again.'

She picks up the mustard suit and one of my mother's food packets, then goes to the kitchen and starts to prepare food. It is as if she's forgotten what she was saying. As she cooks, she begins to unbutton her dress, then pulls it off over her head, exposing her wrinkled flesh. I'm not the kind to look away. I want to see it all, the layered hanging skin, the odd twists of her skeletal deformation where the pelvis is pulled up; the neck and shoulders hang low and the small hump on her back protrudes. The head tries to rebel and hold itself up, but the jowl does not cooperate and gives in to gravity. Mina spreads the mustard skirt on the floor, steps into it and pulls it up to her waist. Putting on the coat requires less ingenuity. She pulls it on and returns to me with more tea. I feel I have to say something.

'I don't remember Sa'i Park as a green place,' I offer. 'I've always seen it as dry, barren and grassless but Baba has shown me photos of it with animal cages and a pond where the swans used to swim. He hides the photo from Maman.'

Mina's eyes are on some other distant memory. 'There was a little man who looked old but was really a child,' she said. 'He came down those steps. He couldn't speak well. He was scared of me. I was afraid of him too. He sat down, hunched over and began pulling up grass. I too sat on the ground but far enough away to not scare him off. I had food in my bag so I took it out and held it in front of me as if I were trying to make friends with a cat. I slowly moved towards him and when I was close enough, he snatched it away and turned his back to me. He dug a hole and buried the food. Occasionally he'd glance over to see if I would object. When he was finally sure I was no threat, he relaxed and began tapping the dirt and smoothing the mound. I pulled up handfuls of grass, took it over, and scattered it over the buried food. He got excited about this and ran around bringing in fistfuls of pulled-up grass to do the same. I gathered a few pebbles and made a beautiful design over the food grave. We were having so much fun but just then a woman rushed down the stairs and grabbed the old boy's hand and dragged him away. I felt utterly dejected. I hung around a bit more, fiddled with the decoration on the grave, then went home.'

I can't believe Mina really remembers all this in such minute detail. No doubt her imagination is lending her story flashy twists. 'Who lived there?' I ask. But it is as if I'm talking to the air.

'I visited him in the following days,' she continues. 'He

had goop-crusted innocent eyes. Our favourite game was to decorate the grave with pebbles. I worried that, in our absence, a passerby might kick and destroy our food grave, so I stuck a long stick in the middle of the mound and tied a green ribbon to it. I think that's what must have saved it because, in the coming days, we found other colourful ribbons tied to the stick, and the grave remained untouched. One time, when a woman came out looking for Bijan, I asked her if she would let him play in the playground. At first, she was hesitant, but eventually she relented and we took him there and let Bijan play. Two or three days later, the woman said the lady of the house, Bijan's mother, wanted to see me. I guess I was kind of stupid because, without a second thought, I followed the woman into the building. His mother wanted to know if I would come to the house sometimes and play with Bijan. She said she'd pay me for it. I liked the idea of money, but I liked Bijan himself even more.'

'And you went, presumably?' I ask.

'I didn't say anything to anyone. I used to go to the house during my study hours. I taught Bijan the alphabet. I played with him. Not out of pity. Sometimes I would take him to the park so that he could see for himself that the food grave was still there.'

'Unbelievable!' I interject. 'You always did like weird things. It's this kind of antics that fuels all the things people say about you behind your back.'

For the first time since she started the story, she looks straight at me and raises her eyebrows. Why do old people have that jelly-like layer on their irises?

'Are they still talking behind my back?' she asks. 'I guess I've become a family proverb. To hell with them! They're just a bunch of bastard idiots running after bread. Who cares? Don't distract me from the story... I taught that kid the alphabet. His name was Bijan. His mum told me I could come into the house and visit him sometimes. She'd pay me. Bijan's hands were not old, but he had these very short nails that were sunken into his flesh. He had these big ears that drooped down. His lips were always chapped. Almost no one visited that house. The floor where Bijan and I spent our time had a large kitchen, a living room and an office where we played. Sometimes the house looked like an abandoned empty palace and once I realised there really was no one else in the house but me and Bijan. Ooof… this story has no tail. When I finally mentioned my visits to the house to my sisters, they said I was bewitched and crazy and that Bijan was a figment of my imagination. The lady of the house told my mother she had seen me only once in the park and that she did not have such a child. And so, decades later, they made a big deal of this reputation of mine, and that's how they managed to cut me off from my own money.'

'So?' I ask. 'Was Bijan real or had you made him up?'

'That's what they said,' Mina replies. 'It was an open and shut case. So, I started to doubt myself too. I thought perhaps I had imagined it all. One day I dragged my mother to the park to show her the food grave so she could see with her own eyes what Bijan and I had built. But the park guard told her that the mound had been there for a very long time and that people say a dervish had sat down and died there, stick in hand and all.'

Looking at Mina, it is as if the guard were right there, speaking those words. Her mother had hit her own head, crying she had lost her child to the spirit world.

I take the tablet from her hands and inspect the photos again. In the ruins, the stairs have cast a shadow on the eastern side of the building. The northern part has been completely destroyed. The other photos show a deep crater that has pulled part of the building into itself.

'OK… so you want to go and see it all up close?' I ask. 'Would it change anything in your mind?'

'It already has,' she says. There is a strange twinkle in her glossy pale eyes, and it frightens me. She goes back to the kitchen. 'It already has,' she repeats.

I've never seen her so unsettled. I wait for her to continue, but she doesn't say anything else. I go to the kitchen and lean against the counter. I clear my throat to get to the point, to unload the result of my own long research. I want to say to her: *Mina Khanum, stop this nonsense; just wait and see what I've got up my sleeve!*

Instead I say: 'Massood Keyvani lost his father when he was fourteen years old. His father had died under suspicious circumstances. The incident changed the course of Keyvani's life because his mother decided she did not want him to remain in Tehran. She sent her son to India where he studied Sanskrit at Bahram Gur University. Sadegh Hedayat,[4] before becoming an acclaimed writer, also studied at that same university. Later, Keyvani went to London but returned to Iran during the Allies' occupation. That's when he realised that the Tehran he had escaped was, in fact, the only place that gave him a sense of purpose. At this point his mother was too old to stop him from remaining in the country, a nation on the verge of a great political upheaval. He had landed right in the middle of it all and wanted to play a role in the events of his time.'

In one of the files related to the incidents of 1953, I had found a copy of a letter attributed to Keyvani. However, the person the letter was addressed to still remained a mystery. 'Shall I read it?' I ask Mina. She says nothing but motions with her hand as if to say, You're going to anyway, so just do it.

Soulat and I stayed up all night waiting for the outcome of the negotiations with the Shah. The night air in the garden was pleasant and, for a change, there was no trace of mosquitoes. Soulat was drunk, as usual, and kept forgetting why we were up and what we were waiting for. When the gate finally opened, I ran to meet the giant American Packard that drove into the courtyard. Soulat was in the same drunken state and had once again forgotten what was going on. The happy faces of the passengers implied that the negotiations with the Shah had gone well. Tomorrow, the Shah would leave for the north of the country. Before his departure, he was going to sign the edict to remove Prime Minister Mosaddegh from his post and appoint a successor. Our work was cut out. By morning, we would have to prepare the text of the directives. Despite the good news, our hearts pounded with concern. We were worried that the Shah might back out of what he had promised to do, or the plot might be leaked, or that old man Mosaddegh may still be up to something. The next day proved that our worries were not unfounded. The Shah had left the city without signing the edicts. One of us had to go to Ramsar to get them signed. I was busy with the bazaar merchants and had an appointment with Habibullah, a carpet merchant, and Abbas Joharchi, the head of the gold merchants' guild, to support the anti-Mosaddegh demonstrations and bring the bazaar merchants out into the streets. As for Soulat, we had little confidence in him. Managing to arrange an appointment with the Shah's people that night was the greatest thing he was able to achieve; beyond that, his periods of sobriety were short. Most times, he drank so much half his head was in this world and half in the next. This was my opinion, but to my surprise they decided to send Soulat to get it done. They argued that since he was on first-name terms with the royal family and was not afraid of a one-on-one debate with his majesty, he would be the best candidate to bring the Shah around and get him to sign the decrees. And so, Soulat went off with the driver in that same American Packard. The next evening, we gathered in the garden and waited. I was pessimistic about the whole affair and was so worried I was unable to eat. Between us, no nail was left unbitten and not a bottle of wine undrunk. Mosaddegh had declared martial law and dissolved the parliament. My mind kept turning like a pinwheel, examining every possible solution. Finally, Soulat returned, triumphant, with a packet containing the signed edicts. Copies of them had to be distributed everywhere and quickly. We went to the Amirabad building to use the stencil machine in the basement. The main decrees of dismissal, appointment, and instructions for the commander of the army had to be immediately delivered to the three principals: Mosaddegh, Zahedi[5] and the commander of the army. I remember that, at some point, they called and woke Soulat up to ask him: 'What secret signal should we assign to the operation?' I could not believe that of all people they had to ask this of Soulat. It was only later I realised there was nothing that perpetually drunk man could not do. Everyone had suggested strange words for the signal, but Soulat, without giving it even a second thought said: 'Tell the radio announcer, instead of saying, "It is midnight," to say: "It is exactly midnight."' In other words, after taking over the radio station, we were supposed to…

'Stop this nonsense,' Mina interrupts, angrily.

'No, Mina,' I say. 'This letter has been verified and…'

'Enough with these idiotic words,' she interrupts again. 'Verification! Don't you see how two or three stupid drunk men apparently divided all the tasks among themselves, and how no other names are mentioned? Enough! I don't want you to read anymore. You're so proud you work in the Office for the Preservation of Documents. You're so stupid you don't even realise the office you work in is, in fact, the office of document-editing and falsifications. Before, the main actors of the story were Americans, now those guys have been erased. The only American character kept in the story is Pacard. Fools! Your story is bullshit from start to finish. Sadegh Hedayat never went to Bahram Gur University.'

'But Keyvani was the main actor in all this,' I protest.

'An insignificant pawn! The real players were others. That code was announced by the BBC to confirm England's support for the coup, and it has nothing to do with that idiot Soulat. How many foreigners work in your office?'

'Why?' I ask. 'What's that got to do with anything?'

'Don't you see? Their main mission is to alter our written history. To erase their own betrayal from all records. In the past, they looted us for oil, now they steal our history. Why do you think they have come here, and now? Afghanistan, Iraq, Jordan… they have taken over the whole region again, but this time in the garb of doctors, sociologists, professors and biologists. They have picked up their pens and erasers and are rewriting our history any which way they want.'

My confidence is knocked by all this but I don't want to give up easily. 'In any case,' I try again, 'thanks to this letter and some other personal notes, following the 1979 revolution Keyvani was accused of treason and disappeared forever, until now, when Tehran uncovered the mystery… I want to write it like this in my report: *Tehran unveils the mystery. Secrets are revealed. The land has been ploughed and once again the ugly face of…* Well, something like that. What do you think?'

Mina looks at me with sad eyes: 'Secrets have been revealed… but isn't it too late? Of all the things you said, that one was a true statement.' She then repeats it: 'Secrets have been revealed.' The jelly over Mina's pupils blurs and dims.

★

On the way to the cable car station, I stop several times just to take in the surroundings. Mina, in her mustard suit and silver hair, introduces a little colour to the grey air. Clara has followed us out. The shadow from her wide-brimmed hat conceals her face, but I know it's her. She points her camera at Mina. 'Mina… Mina,' she says, 'stop right there.' Mina stops but does not look at the camera.

'Doesn't the old station guard mind you taking pictures of him?' I ask. 'Should I check?'

'Take a thousand pictures of the guy,' Mina says indignantly. 'He couldn't care less what the hell anyone does.'

The cable cars are designed in the style of the old one in Tochal,[6] only safer and more high-tech. They're the best way to travel from the mountains north of Tehran to the lower areas. 'Look how much they care about me,' she says. 'They've kept the cable cars going so I can go down whenever I want.'

I say nothing, letting her bask in this fantasy. Earlier, when I had read the letter, she had exuded such intelligence and clear-thinking, and now… such self-delusion. The reason cables cars are protected and serviced is because all government officials, inspectors and scientists reside in these higher developments. Many stations, it's true, were decommissioned but a few, like this one, were kept open and strengthened with concrete reinforcements and pillars firmly drilled into the ground. Mina takes my arm to board the car. I help her into a seat. Clara takes pictures of the old conductor and of us sitting in the car. I make room for Clara between myself and Mina, but she does not board. She photographs us moving away.

The car is empty except for two Japanese men, who despite the available seats, have chosen to stand. They point fingers at the scenery below and talk very fast. Mina is immersed in her own world. If she were paying any attention to me, I would say something funny about the Japanese guys to change the mood and show off my comedic talent. But honestly, I can't think of anything funny to say and Mina's mind is elsewhere anyway. One of the Japanese guys kneels and draws a map on the dusty floor with his finger. He says something in an urgent tone but the other guy just turns his back to him, wags his finger and says: 'No, no, no.' The man gets off his knees and angrily erases the map with the sole of one shoe. He then goes to the door of the cable car, grabs the handle and freezes.

From up here, I can see the cable along which we move, a languid line that links Tajrish Square to the Railway Square; the mountain to the unstable clay of the Deadlands. Years ago, when the 'second edition' of that map was leaked and passed from hand to hand, people started calling these places 'deadlands' because that was the term written beside each cross-hatched area on the map. Thanks to the map, those living outside these marked areas felt safer. We too now live well outside those cross-hatched areas. Maman hates our house in Semnan, so Baba is building a new house on the Shahroud plot. We originally moved to the Semnan house in a hurry when Maman's office building collapsed right before her eyes. She was standing outside the building waiting for a friend, when a hole opened up and the entire building vanished like a nail hammered into the ground. The force of it threw my mother several metres away and she saw trees uprooted, peeling back the skin of the earth. We fled Tehran that very night.

'Do you remember how we left Tehran?' I ask Mina.

But Mina's mind is somewhere else. 'Where do you think the owners went when the building became the Clock Museum?' she asks.

'I guess they themselves must have sold the building to the Cultural Heritage Department' I speculate.

'I never knew how old Bijan was, but if he is still alive...' she muses, 'he probably still looks the same. He always looked old. He'd be younger than me, much younger.'

'Why was everyone so insistent that the boy didn't exist?' I ask.

'His existence was beside the point,' she says. 'They claimed I'd lost my marbles and that it was all in my head. The lady who took care of Bijan, the one who used to pick him up at the park, swore blind that she had seen me only once or twice at the park, and that I had always been alone. This freaked my mother out. She sent me far away from here because she couldn't come to terms with the possibility that her daughter was possessed and talking gibberish. I had been in that house more than ten times. But they wouldn't even let me go into the study to look for Bijan's toys. They wouldn't even let me talk. They kept looking at me with pity, saying I had totally lost my mind.'

'You hadn't imagined it all?' I ask again. 'Honestly?'

'I began to think that maybe I had; that I really was

missing a few marbles in my head.'

This is where we would both laugh and I'd say, 'Well, you kinda are, Mina.' But she does not laugh, and I refrain from being a smartass. 'You know what happens when you truly believe you're nuts?' she says. 'It liberates you; gives you permission to do whatever the hell you want because you supposedly don't have a reasonable mind to prevent you from doing crazy stuff.'

When we arrive, the Japanese guy holding the door handle jumps out and leaves as if suddenly released from a cage, but the other one is glued to the bench and seems to have no intention of getting off. I take Mina's arm and lead her to the door. She can't step off and down, so I pick her up and lower her onto the station platform. She is light as a feather.

'What was with those guys?' I ask.

'Which guys?' she wonders.

Some of the electric sidewalks on both sides of the main street are still in operation. I had imagined we would ride them all way to Sa'i Park, but now, I see stretches of them have stopped running. We walk down a steep street that used to be called Gandhi Road. A guard in red uniform asks to see our passage cards. He warns that the street is not safe and that we are better off taking a rickshaw. Mina doesn't want to ride in a rickshaw. I don't care if we do or not. These rickshaw pullers are neither descendants of ancient Hindus nor dwarfs who have popped out of the earth — a story that became a Tehran urban legend, whispered among the new capital's residents. The truth is, these unfortunate men are from that lowest rung of society, forced to do the hard labour in every era of human history. Men with thin, muscular arms, sunburnt faces, wrinkled foreheads and eyes that are forever asking: 'For how long?'

One such man takes us to the park. He runs down Gandhi Road so fast it's as if he has no brakes and is about to lose control, topple and send both Mina and I to the ever-after. Mina dying this way would be hilarious. I mean, after so much persistence, surviving, and waiting to see Tehran return to itself, for her to simply end up in pieces on this street and be forgotten for good. But the rickshaw finally slows down and lets us off a bit short of the park. Mina's colour has disappeared from her face. I wait a bit to let her catch her breath, but she keeps staring at her shoes as if she doesn't want to take another step. I give her a bottle of water. She takes a sip and says: 'I went there a lot. Ten times, at least. One time, Bijan was hungry and no matter how much I called out to the maid, she never came. So, I went to the kitchen and looked in the fridge to see what I could find. Suddenly the tall cabinet next to the fridge opened and out came an old man in a crimson gown with golden cuffs. When he saw me, he froze and stared at me with his big eyes. I thought, here is another Bijan; maybe this is a house where old men – who really are children – hide in cabinets. I grabbed a piece of bread and got the hell out of there. A few minutes later, I returned to the kitchen but there was no sign of the man. I searched all the cabinets. Nothing. When the maid finally showed up, I asked: "Who was the old man in the kitchen?"'

Now, I'm thinking maybe Mina is as crazy as others say. I love her and have always defended her against those who bad-mouth her, but now she's pushing it. Why is she dredging up this nonsense from her childhood years, when we are so close to the hideout of one the most notorious agents of the 1953 coup? What does it matter if Bijan was real or not? Maybe he was just an odd child his parents kept hidden away. I take Mina's hand and almost drag her towards the site.

It's as if someone has taken a sharp knife and carved sections of the road out. They have cordoned off the site with a rope and no one is allowed to go past. Scaffolding has been erected to install large tents to shelter the photographers, reporters and artists who will be capturing and documenting the site. The street, the mansion, and the Sa'i Park stairs have all split open like a clean cut to reveal a subterranean structure.

The upper floors are abandoned and in ruin, but the basement has remained intact. It is tidy and colourful. The great hall has suffered a cut along its length, and the carpet, the dining table and the leather sofa have been sliced exactly in half. Several large statues stand sentry and a brass samovar sits on a small table that has been placed against the wall as if readied for guests. I think they have dusted and arranged them like that. I ask a guy if that's the case, and he says no. There is no sign of Keyvani's grave. Maybe when the building collapsed, he was buried all over again. But then again, how did they find his bones? The basement has no doors or windows, nor any stairs connecting it anywhere. But the remains of metal parts from a hydraulic pulley have the technicians guessing that there may have been an elevator hidden somewhere between the walls or inside utility spaces, or something like that, connecting the basement to the upper floor. I have completely forgotten Mina. She is standing on this side of the rope, utterly stunned, staring at the basement. I feel sorry for her, so I go over, take her hand.

'Are you OK?' I ask.

I'm worried about her. I think maybe she has had enough, and we should return home. I look at the steep road and wonder how I'm going to get her back up there when I see Carla standing in front of a rickshaw puller, taking photos of him. Mina looks at me, eyes sparkling with joy

'I was not bewitched!' she says. 'There really was a Bijan!' She points a trembling finger at the basement and stutters: 'That... old man... was also a Keyvan. The one that... came out from the cabinet... next to the fridge. In a crimson robe!'

'The old man?...'

I suddenly sense that history has reared its head right before my eyes. These people who are moving about, turning over every rock, taking bones to the laboratory, trying to figure out what connected the basement to the rest of the house, don't even know that living history is right here, staring them in the face.

'I shouldn't have seen him,' she says. 'But I did, and that's why they called me crazy. So that no one would believe anything I said.'

'But what did Bijan have to do with any of this?'

Mina shakes her head, speechless. I try to connect the dots: 'When everyone testified you were making up this kid, Bijan, it officially established your insanity. That way, if you later said something about the old man, they would just point at your record of mental instability and say you should be locked up in a loony bin. What a horrible thing they did... to you, just a sixteen-year-old kid! Oh, Mina, Mina... God help me, I too thought you were crazy. I pretended to be on your side, but in my heart of hearts... no, I can't say it... but I must... It was them I believed.'

My throat is dry, and I can't continue. I just stand there next to Mina staring ahead. Mina's hand trembles in mine. 'After all these years...' she murmurs, 'I wish my mother was here to see it. I wish my daughter...'

From the volume of operations being conducted around the site, it is clear they intend to build something like a museum here. Mina says, 'They are busy fabricating a new story. Mark my words, soon this building will be drained of its history.'

A strong gust of wind suddenly cools the air. I put my arm around Mina and the back of my neck begins to tingle as if someone is watching us. I turn my head and look. I see someone looking at us, the 'us' inside a Jacek Yerka painting: A young man with his arm around an old woman in a mustard skirt and coat, her silver hair pulled to one side. They stand in front of a pit. The woman stares at a collapsed building on the other side, the basement of which, with its chandelier and red cushions, is undamaged. The young man is looking straight at the viewer as if he has always known this moment would be captured, mounted in an ornate frame, and hung in a museum.

Notes

1. Tajrish Square, also known as Sar-e Pol-e Tajrish (at the Tajrish Bridge), is actually a vast bridge on top of a qanat waterway. As a Tehran neighbourhood, it sits to the northeast of the city centre.
2. Ancient, underground aqueducts or man-made watercourses.
3. The last Iranian royal dynasty that ruled for roughly 53 years between 1925 and 1979.
4. Sadegh Hedayat (1903-1951) was an Iranian writer, poet and translator. Best known for his novel *The Blind Owl*, he was one of the earliest Iranian writers to adopt literary modernism.
5. Fazlollah Zahedi (1892-1963) was an Iranian military officer and statesman who replaced the Iranian Prime Minister Mohammad Mosaddegh through a CIA and MI5-led coup d'état of 1953.
6. Tochal is a mountain and ski resort located on the Alborz mountain range, adjacent to the metropolitan area of Tehran.

Staring into the Void

Ebrahim Farrokh

Translated by Jim Preacher

To the Javid-Naman[1] of Zahedan's Bloody Friday[2]

1.

THIS STORY IS ABOUT darkness, or the future, or perhaps a combination of the two. At that particular moment, however, Rahman knew nothing of such things.

As usual, Rahman was setting out after work to catch some shut-eye in that small, damp room of his, when suddenly, having barely left his office, he fell into a temporal void. At first, he was engulfed by darkness. He feared he might be dead and felt like he was being suffocated. Then a sense of weightlessness washed over him and his body began to ascend through the darkness. As his eyes adjusted and his body continued to rise, he began to notice the faint outline of figures approaching him. The moments that followed were unlike any he had ever experienced. But when one of the other workers pulled him up from the void the next morning, Rahman couldn't remember any of those unearthly moments that he had experienced.

Arriving at work the next day, Rahman's boss wanted to hurl abuse at him, but then his eyes fell on the dark hole that was clinging to the ground next to the silo like an octopus and slowly increasing in size. He angrily instructed the workers to place blocks of lead around the temporal void until the officers arrived. Though his boss didn't want to accept it, what had happened to Rahman was not a particularly rare thing anymore. It had been several years since temporal voids first began sprouting out of nowhere and swallowing up unfortunate passersby. No one knew why: some attributed it to atomic radiation from past explosions, while others thought it could be the result of increased solar radiation. Those who returned alive from inside the voids would report vivid dreams and distorted images. Many believed that the images meant something. The government thought the same, though no one knew what they had managed to figure out. One thing was clear, however: they did not like the voids, nor the victims who survived them.

It seemed the officers who soon arrived at the site and began dragging Rahman away didn't like him either. They blindfolded him, then beat him, insulted him, and dumped his battered body by a track on the outskirts of the city.

When Rahman limped back to the worksite late that night, there was no trace of the temporal void, save for a lead dome. He encountered his boss, who didn't even have the energy to berate him like he usually would. It seemed the officers had got their point across to him, too. He handed a digital letter over to Rahman. In a dry and threatening tone, the letter instructed him to visit a specialist's office the next day, with no further explanation.

Rahman already knew what would happen to him if he failed to show up. He held the projection panel aloft. A box for his fingerprint appeared. He pressed his finger on the box and the words on the hologram were replaced with the address of the office he was to attend. He folded the panel and placed it in his pocket. His boss then signalled that he was free to leave.

The office was located on the third floor of a building in the city centre; close to the ministry building but not actually part of it. Upon entering the office, Rahman felt troubled by its facade of complete normality – it felt like they had deliberately tried to disguise it. He only began to relax after noticing the vast, orderly array of camera lenses that were monitoring him. He said hello and, after seeking permission, he sat with a straight back on the snug, black sofa, beside a peculiar-looking machine. He stared down at the floor. He didn't dare look up, but from the corner of his eye he could tell that the consultant behind the desk felt even more uncomfortable than he did. The consultant tapped the table twice. 'Mr Malek-Zahi?' he asked. 'Rahman Malek-Zahi? Are you paying attention to me, Mr Malek-Zahi?'

Rahman raised his head instinctively. He tried his best to ignore the cameras watching him. The consultant looked at him anxiously. He was a middle-aged man with a slight potbelly, wearing a chequered, short-sleeved shirt and jam-jar glasses. He was balding at the front but had still retained most of his grey hair. Overall, it appeared that time had been kind to him, but he seemed scared that one mistake could cost him everything he had ever worked for. 'Mr Malek-Zahi?' he repeated.

'Yes, Mohandes,'[3] Rahman replied. 'Yes, sorry. I'm a bit… confused.'

'That's only natural,' the man continued. 'Especially after what you've been through – it's natural. But please don't call me Mohandes; it makes me feel awkward. My name is Saghaei. Javid Saghaei. But please call me Javid, and I will call you Rahman, if that's alright with you?'

'Whatever you think best, Mohandes.'

Javid tapped the mod behind his ear. Rahman couldn't see anything, but he could tell from the glint in the pupil of his eye that Javid was using a mod. Javid paused for a moment then spoke:

'Rahman, I've looked everywhere but can't find any trace of your identification number in the archives. Simply put, you don't exist in the system. Is there any particular reason for that?'

'Well, I am Baloch,[4] Mohandes,' Rahman explained. 'The government won't give us identification numbers. I tried to apply for one but they keep dragging their heels. I don't know why – God only knows. They won't let me get one of those earpieces either – if an officer spots me without one, I'll be in big trouble.'

Javid offered a faint smile but suddenly diverted his attention to the camera above their heads, monitoring them both.

'Yes, of course,' he said nervously. 'There are some complications, just like everywhere else in the world. But it will work out. Officials are certainly considering…'

'Yes, yes. We always put our faith in God first, and our hope in the authorities. For sure, they have our best interests at heart and care…' Now it was Rahman's turn to look warily at the camera from the corner of his eye.

'Well, Rahman,' Javid interrupted, 'I don't want to take up any more of your time. Let's get started. Do you have anything metallic on your person? You don't have a mod installed?'

Rahman placed his hand on the table and the metal penholder slowly began to rise in the air. It span around and settled in the palm of Rahman's hand.

Javid nodded: 'Metallokinesis?'

'What, Mohandes?'

Javid paused to explain. 'Errrm, the colloquial term would be "metalsmithing". Those things they implanted under your knuckles and palms, for manipulating and shaping metal. That's what they installed in your hands, right?'

'Uhuh, Mohandes,' Rahman replied. 'I don't know about no metal-whatever… They used the same word you did, Mohandes. You get this great pain that goes through your hand when you use them…'

'Bastards…' Javid muttered angrily and impulsively under his breath.

'What's that, Mohandes?'

'Nothing… nothing. It's just… you know, your hands and fingers will become deformed if you use those mods too much. They'll disfigure you. You'll lose your hand. If I were you, I'd find another job…'

Rahman grinned. 'You must be joking, Mohandes.'

Javid nodded. He didn't want to press the issue any further. The cameras were staring at him. 'Could you stand in front of the machine, please?'

Rahman complied. Javid also walked over and stood behind the machine:

'Bend over a little. Place both of your hands on the pads. Lean on it. Don't be afraid to put all of your weight on it. Do you know what this machine is for? Have you seen one of these before?'

Rahman shook his head.

'A somnogram… that is, a dream visualiser… it's called a dream visualiser.' Javid repeated. 'You hook it up to a person's head, and you can see their dreams. You know, I have other clients besides you. Some of them are sent by their psychiatrist because they suffer from depression or anxiety, you know — things like that. Although those who come of their own accord aren't much better off. They come to review their dreams. They're searching for greater meaning, for a sign: a sign that might provide an escape route. But dreams don't give you that. But… But, in your case…'

Javid slammed his hands on the machine. Rahman flinched and jumped backwards. Javid immediately apologised: 'Sorry… Sorry… I got a little excited. What I mean is… people like you, as in, people who have fallen into a temporal void — their minds interpret what they see there as a dream. We don't know why. There is a theory about it. They say it relates to the brain's interpretation of quantum and multidimensional space. Let's move on. Could you take your shirt off, please?'

Rahman paused, as if ashamed to remove his shirt, before

reluctantly undoing each button, one after the other. He scrunched the shirt up in his hand and threw it on the floor by his feet.

A black, void-like bubble covered most of his chest. Pure black. It was like peering into an aquarium and seeing bright, shimmering particles that resemble stars in the night sky. 'A Dirac hole. Erm, could you… touch it with your hand?' Javid asked.

Rahman nodded. He placed his hand gently on the rim of the hole and pulled it down.

'You can't really touch it, of course,' Javid said. 'There's nothing there. At least, not something that can be touched by a hand. A Dirac hole, the thing in the middle of your chest, is something that exists between dimensions. In fact, it's your mind that makes you think there's something there to be touched. It's your mind that creates that illusion.'

'Mohandes, what are you…' Rahman cut himself off mid-sentence. Fear had stolen the air from his lungs. Javid towered above him, a pair of protective goggles covering his eyes and a proton gun in each hand. Sparks flared from the coiled ends of the gun barrels. 'It'll all be over before you feel a thing,' he smiled reassuringly.

Javid abruptly thrust the gun barrels into the void of Rahman's chest. The guns discharged a large spark upon first contact with the hole. All of the electricity in the room cut out for a moment before promptly returning. Then, through the neural pathway of the wires running from the gun to his arm, his mind entered Rahman's consciousness.

First, Javid saw a tall pillar – taller than anything he could imagine – as tall as the darkness that had surrounded him. Inch by inch, his gaze travelled down the lead surface of the pillar. At the bottom sat Rahman. Right at the very bottom. Javid couldn't see him clearly, but it must have been Rahman; he recognised him from his clothing and the frozen shape of his body.

Rahman cupped his ears. He could hear something: the

sound of hissing smoke, the sound of firecrackers, and then the stench of burnt tar. It was all consistent with other reports and cases that Javid had observed. They weren't all identical, but together they seemed to paint a larger picture. A picture of what? Javid still hadn't figured that out.

When Rahman regained consciousness, Javid was busy reviewing the footage on a tablet connected to the machine. As he picked up his crumpled shirt from the floor, Javid asked him if he wanted to watch the video. Rahman responded with a firm 'no'. He asked for permission to leave the office before promptly doing so. Rahman hoped that he would never have to set foot in there again.

2.

But Rahman's hope was in vain. Only a month later, he was called back to the same office. Javid's face was awash with anguish, in stark contrast to the men who had dragged Rahman from his workplace and given him a thorough beating on the way there.

Rahman had not yet taken a seat when Javid nervously remarked, 'Look, I swear to God, I wouldn't have let them haul you back here if it were up to me. I don't know what they're afraid of... Sorry, they're not afraid — they're just concerned. Some of those poor souls have fallen into the voids themselves. They haven't caused too much trouble. Look, between us...'

He glanced at the camera above his head then leaned forward and continued: 'Well, not just between us... I'm going to level with you. They don't know this themselves. I have no choice, sir. I have no choice. There are no experts in this field. I have to do this to keep my work permit.'

He paused for a moment. He clasped his hands together and continued: 'Look. Remember that machine from last time?'

'Yes, Mohandes,' Rahman replied. 'I wanted to ask you about that, to be honest. It's gone. Did you get rid of it?'

Javid scratched his chin.

'Yes. Well, no,' he replied. 'The machine is in the next room. They've completely changed the system, and it seems that more things can be picked up with the new one. Anyone who's ever fallen into a void has been forced to come back once again. One of them was an old man. It was years ago that he fell into one, but they forced him back here. When he arrived here yesterday, he'd gone completely pale. He was afraid that he might be in trouble. You know what I mean. I reassured him and explained that he wasn't the only one – that everyone was being called back – until he finally calmed down. Anyway, let's get going, I don't want to take up any more of your time.' He held out his hand. 'Shall we?'

Rahman looked around the room, confused. His eyes fell on a door that he was sure hadn't been there the last time. The door was metal and completely black, trimmed with yellow hazard warning tape. 'Whatever you say, Mohandes.'

'Good,' Javid replied. 'Just don't throw your shirt on the floor like last time, please. Take it off and hang it… no, that'll be too much trouble for you. Just leave it on my table. There are some gloves on the table as well – please put them on.'

Rahman complied. He unfastened the buttons on his shirt and placed it on the table. The cameras followed Javid as he made his way towards the door. He held his wrist up in front of the camera at the door. It flashed and the door opened. He glanced back at Rahman, who hadn't budged from his place.

'Is something troubling you?'

'No, Mohandes. I'm just feeling homesick.'

'Do you have a wife?' Javid asked. 'Kids?'

'Aye, she's my cousin. Two kids: a girl and a boy. It's been a year since I last saw them. I miss them.'

'I understand,' Javid replied. 'I have a daughter myself. Children are the light of your life. I always keep a picture of her here. Inside the mod. I can't bear to be away from her for one second. I must say, your hand… it's got worse.'

'It's nothing, Mohandes,' Rahman insisted.

The new room they walked into was a blinding shade of white, from floor to ceiling. At the centre of it stood an aquarium, inside which was a bright, glowing, human-shaped figure. But it wasn't entirely human. The body was floating in the clear liquid. The aquarium's lid resembled a placenta with a cluster of wires extending out of it, all of which were connected directly to the top of an empty bed in the middle of the room.

'The problem with the previous machine,' Javid began, 'was that it would automatically collate the data and we could only see what it had selected for us. But it's more important to have a collection of everything the dreamer feels, rather than just what they see. Now we can have it all. Let me put it another way. A century ago, perhaps, people thought that dreams had some meaning behind them: a manifestation of repressed desires, and things that you couldn't come to terms with. That is one part of it, for sure… oh.' He stopped himself. 'Could you lie down on the bed, please?'

Rahman complied and lay flat on the bed. 'So, what am I going to see, Mohandes?' he asked.

'I don't know,' Javid replied. 'A feeling, or an outline of something that hasn't happened yet. Whatever it may be, your mind won't be able to comprehend it. Probably because it's not the right time.'

As he finished speaking, a mask locked in place around Rahman's face. Javid tapped it then gently lowered two separate wires into the sea of stars in Rahman's chest – a sea that had grown larger since last time.

Javid nervously lit a cigarette, despite the fact he didn't even smoke. Immediately regretting his decision, he put the cigarette out. He still couldn't face reality. He stepped aside, and leaned against the casing of the aquarium, half collapsing. He didn't know why he had lied about his daughter, especially now that all was lost. He thought about the future. It's strange how you only think about the future when there is no future; when the only thing you can see is darkness. Javid wanted to feel the light. He wanted to feel the warmth. So, he grabbed the only thing within reach. He bowed his head and used the cable to connect to the aquarium – to connect to Rahman's mind.

The inside of Rahman's mind was murky and dry, with a wind as hot as a furnace that seared through to the deepest layers of Javid's skin. A yellow haze seemed to have cast a curtain over everything – a kind of stifling yellow that had even discoloured the green leaves of what few trees were around. The asphalt on the street was old and full of cracks. There was no sign of anyone, as far as he could see, but the sound of commotion was still echoing in the distance. He could make out another sound, however, amongst all the uproar. Someone was singing. Javid didn't understand what was being sung, but he recognised the accent with its melodic and high-pitched timbre, and words that seemed to stretch on for an eternity. The voice was pained but not sorrowful. Javid began to feel a lump in his throat.

Rahman awoke. 'Thank you,' Javid said. Rahman didn't understand why, but he nodded and left.

3.

Three years passed before they saw each other again. By that time, Rahman's hands were shaking uncontrollably, though the mod had not yet completely destroyed them. Entering the office again, he was taken aback. It was pitch black and at first he thought that he had entered the wrong room. But as he turned to leave, Javid's voice drew him back in: 'You're in the right place, my friend… I'm a little… I'm not quite feeling like myself. Would you take a seat?'

Rahman sat down.

'Do you know why you're here today?' Javid continued.

'No, Mohandes,' Rahman replied. 'The officers treated me better this time, but they also seemed angrier in a way.'

'I want to tell you a story,' Javid said. 'Would you like to hear it?'

'Well, Mohandes…'

'What I want to tell you is important. It's better that you hear it.'

'Whatever you think is best,' Rahman offered.

Javid paused. He pushed his chair back but then leaned forward and began the story:

'Once upon a time, a group of people in this land began building a bomb. The most terrifying bomb you could imagine. A bomb that could instantly wipe an entire city off the face of the earth – an atomic bomb and all the terrible things that come with it. Everyone knew it was there, but the group just denied it. They lied. They said there was no bomb, right as they were assembling it in the darkest corners. But then those same people were removed from power. What I'm talking about took place almost a century ago. Those who succeeded looked everywhere for the bomb but they could never find it. Eventually, they started to wonder if the bomb had been a lie. Maybe the previous regime had been telling the truth. Maybe there was never a bomb to begin with…'

'But no,' Javid shouted suddenly. 'The bomb was there… miles underground, in the furthest depths imaginable. It was ready to explode and its radioactive discharge would warp and distort our reality. The bomb is still there. It is the bomb's residual radiation that creates the temporal voids. It bends time and space. I think that what you saw, what others see, is the future. And at some point, somewhere, that future will align with the present. How and why? I still don't know.'

Javid paused for a moment, leaning back. 'I'm telling you these things,' he continued, 'because I think…you have a right to know. I know you feel uneasy. It's natural for you to feel uneasy towards a government lapdog like me. But I like to think that I've changed. I'm telling you this for your sake and for my own safety. I'm going to switch the electricity back on now. Don't breathe a word about what I've just told you. Don't even hint that you know a thing.'

Rahman nodded. The lights came on. All of the cameras turned violently towards Javid. He smiled, paying no attention to the cameras. His face looked gaunt beneath his thick, untrimmed beard. 'Right, do you know why you're here?' he asked.

'No, Mohandes. Has something happened?'

'The machines have been updated. God willing, I think they should help bring your case to a close this time. Shall we proceed?'

Rahman nodded. He began unbuttoning his shirt but his hand was shaking. His fingers wouldn't work properly. Every button would slip between his fingers and unfastening each one was an agonising struggle.

'Look, I'll take your shirt,' Javid said, snatching it away the moment Rahman had finished removing it. 'It's just, your hand... has it got worse?'

'Yes, Mohandes.'

'I told you, the work you do...'

'Mohandes, that's none of your business...' Rahman snapped, turning around angrily and heading towards the exit. Before reaching the door, however, he seemed to have a change of heart. He turned back again, 'What am I supposed to do about my wife and children?' he asked. 'Let them go hungry? Is that part of God's plan, Mohandes? I just have to get on with it.' He paused, then continued, 'Anyway, Mohandes, the sooner we get this over with, the better.'

Javid nodded in agreement, and headed towards the other door.

'Oh, by the way, your daughter...' Rahman asked.

'There's nothing to say. She's gone...' Javid replied.

Rahman took the hint and didn't press the subject any further.

When they entered the room, there was no trace of the aquarium or the plain white walls. A single, folding bed stood in the middle of the room. The room itself, however, resembled a cage of microchips patched together, piece by piece, through electronic circuits. Each one was connected to the bed by a wire. It looked like the web of a spider entangling its prey. Rahman felt stifled and suffocated by it, but he held himself together and lay down on it.

Javid didn't wait around. He left the room and stood by the panel. He waited for the indicator lights to turn green before immediately jacking into the panel.

This time he didn't see anything. He could feel the dryness in his throat, the warmth of the sun on his skin, the burning pain in his side and his ribs. The stench of sunburn filled his mind with all kinds of stimuli. Javid couldn't take anymore. He unplugged himself. He ran his hand through his hair and sat down beside the wall, trying to hold back tears. He didn't understand any of it and had no interest in trying to. The newer machines just confused him. The cameras looked at him impishly. He felt like the man behind the camera was laughing at him.

When Rahman left, Javid hoped that he would never see him again.

4.

Six years had passed since Rahman last saw Javid at that office. In the midday summer heat, Rahman stood by the metal-working machine in the warehouse, trembling despite being soaked in sweat. He could no longer clench his fists. He tried to screw the metal mould onto the machine. Straining to bend his fingers even slightly, he gestured with his hands to turn the mould. He attempted to bend it a little further but the pain permeated through every inch of him.

He fell to the ground, wailing. Tears welled up in his eyes.

As the pain began to subside, his attention was drawn to the sound of arguing and swearing coming from outside. Suddenly he heard a voice that he never expected to hear again.

Outside, his boss Haji[5] was grappling with Javid and repeatedly pushing and shoving him. 'You lowlife scum!' Haji was yelling. 'I know your kind better than anyone. Not every government agent needs a badge and uniform!'

'Sir…'

'Quit your yapping!' Haji snapped. 'You show up in this run-down slum, with a face like that, looking for some Afghan? Do I look like an idiot?'

'Haj Aqa,' Rahman intervened. 'I'm not Afghan. And I know Mr Javid.'

Haji let go of Javid's collar and turned angrily towards Rahman: 'So, you know him. And what the fuck are you doing here? You worthless slacker, what have you stopped working for? To come and snitch to your little agent friend? You bum. Look here…'

Javid tapped on Haji's shoulder: 'I already told you, sir. I'll cover the cost.'

Haji grabbed Javid's wrist firmly and stared into his face: 'Not so fast. That's not how things are done around here. You think I'll front the cost? No way, man. I'm losing money here. Whatever you're offering needs to be worth my while…'

'Haj Aqa,' Javid tried again. 'I'll cover the cost however best suits you.'

Upon hearing this, Haji nodded in approval and began to haggle. Once the negotiations were concluded, Javid approached Rahman: 'Rahman, let's go…'

'Where, Mohandes?'

'The office.'

'Why?'

'Look, you don't need to call me Mohandes all the time. Please call me Javid…'

'Why, Mr Javid?'

'Because it's vital.'

'You should've sent the officers to collect me like usual. You didn't have to come here yourself…'

'Look, the officers don't know. I mean, they mustn't know. I'll explain on the way.'

'No, Mohandes.'

'No?'

'No, Mr Javid. Whatever it is, you have to tell me right here, right now.'

Javid paused. He scratched the back of his head nervously. Finally, he spoke up:

'Right, remember what I told you about the bomb? The bomb that created the voids. We are… fighting against it.'

'The bomb?'

Javid hesitated. He couldn't find the right words for what he wanted to say. 'Yes, the bomb,' he continued eventually. 'Let me put it this way, all of those temporal voids – all of the things that people saw when they fell into them – are connected to one another. They're telling the story of a moment from the future. Something is going to happen. A great uprising. The more the dreamers experience those moments, the more people advance towards that future, and the bomb starts to decay. But the government doesn't want that to happen. They don't want the future to exist. That's why they're recalling all of the machines. They are protecting the bomb. Because they know that if the bomb is gone, there will be a future…'

'And?' Rahman asked.

'Something must be…'

'No,' Rahman interrupted, 'what does it have to do with us, Mr Javid? My son is dead. My hands don't work. My wife and child are hungry. I have no life. There's nothing more for me to give. I can't. I'm not your man, Mr Javid. I'm not your man.'

Javid wanted to respond, but he bit his tongue. He sat on the ground, beneath the torrid glare of the sun, and gazed at the distant vista of Tehran. It was a warm, late summer afternoon. A gentle breeze swept through the air, but it wasn't strong enough to overpower the blistering sunlight on their skin, nor the layers of dried sweat.

Rahman also looked out at the city, wrapped in fog like a cocoon. The city reflected his own anguish – just as wretched and gloomy. 'Mr Javid, can I tell you about my son?' Rahman asked.

'Yes, please feel free.'

'He was sixteen years old. I went straight back to my hometown when they told me that he was dead. I had to collect the body. The sight of his body horrified me. They'd beaten him to death. He was young and rebellious, I thought to myself. He must have been trying to act tough, and they beat him up for it. I knew that an officer had killed him. But his friends told me a different story. Some officers had grabbed him by the scruff of the neck late one night. They mocked him. But the poor child bowed his head and didn't say a word. That just spurred them on more. They started hitting him and, at some point, his head got slammed into a wall and he died. Mohandes, I mean Mr Javid, please can you tell me what sin mankind has to atone for? Why is there no justice? Is God angry? What crime have we wretched souls committed to deserve this suffering?'

Javid nodded. 'I don't know,' he said. 'I've thought about it a lot. But I really don't know.'

'What about your daughter, Mr Javid? How did you get over the pain?'

'I never got over it. I don't think I'll ever get over it or be able to talk about it, but…' Javid stopped. The intense sunlight beamed directly on him. The sorrow in his eyes was veiled by the blinding glare of his glasses.

'I dream about her,' he went on. 'Not every night, but most nights. I know that dreams don't have any specific meaning. But behind all that meaninglessness is our anger, our sorrow, our future. And they, the government and their agents, want to take that future away from us with their bomb. I can't let them get away with it anymore.'

5.

The two of them got in the car. The warehouse was located a short distance off the main road to Karaj. Javid's car struggled to traverse the rocky trail, but after ten minutes, they finally reached the main road. Following that, it was a half-hour drive to Tehran. After turning onto Azadi Street, they reached the winding, multi-levelled streets of Tehran. First, down Shekari Street by Ekbatan Town, then on to Sattar Khan. Every street name had significance. Blood had been spilt on every one of them in the name of liberty; it sank through the cracks in the asphalt, under the sickly glow of the countless neon lights. Rahman looked out. He could see the sunken faces in the shadows. He saw the silent anger in their eyes. He saw the throbbing pulse of anger in every brick and kerb – in every flicker of the lights.

After arriving at Jomhouri Runway, their car took flight alongside the other vehicles. Javid felt rejuvenated. He could see the glistening of lights and the crowd below, but there was something unusual about it. The crowd was not moving. Everyone was standing still and looking upwards. He didn't understand why, but he could feel it. He could feel the pulse of change. Then he looked back down and saw that the crowd had finally begun to move.

Javid landed his car on the roof of the building. Keeping the lights off as they went, they both made their way down the stairs and towards the office. Once they were both inside, Javid pushed the table against the door and activated the electronic lock.

Rahman looked at the cameras. Javid had smashed most of them – the rest he had blinded with spray paint. The lights came on and within a minute they heard shouting coming from behind the door: 'Open up!'

The officer banged on the door and unleashed a flood of obscenities. They moved on to the next room. Javid closed the iron door behind Rahman.

The room was dark at first, but then it began to light up, little by little. Rahman was flabbergasted. What surrounded him made him feel as if he were among the stars of the midnight sky. 'The thing is, these aren't stars...' Javid remarked. 'What you're seeing is the interaction of electric charges...'

'The what of what, Mohandes?'

'Nothing. Nothing. Let's sit down.'

They sat together with their backs leant against the wall. They could still hear the dull, muffled yelling on the other side of the door. Javid stuck his hand in his pocket and pulled out a small controller about the size of a thimble. 'Take this,' he said. 'Put it behind your ear.'

'Is that it?' Rahman asked in surprise.

'That's it.'

Rahman took the controller, and placing it behind his ear, he immediately fainted. Javid looked away from Rahman and gazed at the infinity of stars inside the room. The sounds of swearing grew fainter and fainter in Javid's mind. He sneered at the camera above him. He could almost feel the rage emanating from behind the camera. In his heart, he felt victorious. He stared at the darkness before him, at a future that had not yet arrived, at a sadness that would never heal – just like the void in Rahman's chest: just as dark, with stars just as bright. He reflected on all the moments and decisions that had led him to that room. He thought about himself and the sky before him, in defiance of the bomb, in defiance of the whole world. 'Was it all worth it?' he asked himself. But he had already answered that question long ago. It was worth it.

Rahman slowly began to regain consciousness. The controller fell from behind his ear. He opened his eyes and leant against the wall.

'What happened then?' Javid asked. 'What did you see?'

'Didn't you see, Mr Javid?' Rahman replied.

'No. The new device doesn't let me do that.'

'Well, it was midday,' Rahman began. 'We were back in my hometown. There was a crowd that stretched back as far as the eye could see. The sun was shining in our eyes. We were yelling. We even threw a few stones. There was anger. We were met with bullets and batons from the other side. It suddenly got dark, but the sun was still out. The street was full of dead bodies, and the blood poured down on our heads and faces. But we wouldn't give up. We kept going higher and higher. And Mr Javid, you were right! The bomb was right there. The bastard had hidden itself in the darkness. But the officers knew about it. They knew damn well.'

'Then what?' Javid asked.

'They separated us from the crowd. They tied me to a pole. The pole was tall – so tall that it reached the heavens. I was hanging there, extremely thirsty, with my hands tied. There was a glass of water in front of me. The officers were laughing. I started singing. I sang of my sorrow. Of my anger. The officers were caught off guard…'

'And after that?' Javid pressed.

'There was no after that. I don't think I survived. I'd been hit by two bullets – right here on my left side. But I could feel them in that darkness. People like me. People like you. They were all there. People who knew that the bomb was there. This might sound strange, but it can be defeated. The voids are a sign. We just need to get out of here somehow.'

Javid pointed at the door: 'That's the way out, over there.'

'But Mr Javid, there's an officer…'

'No,' Javid reassured him 'He's not there anymore. You can open the door and see for yourself. But this is the end of the line for me. Where you're going, I can't follow.'

Rahman was perplexed but he decided to stand up. He walked over to the door and opened it. He immediately recognised the darkness that had engulfed the frame of the door: a temporal void.

'The thing about the voids,' Javid called out, 'is that they're not just a window into the future. They're a rift in time and space. When you enter one, you don't know where you'll end up afterwards – you don't know if you'll be able to get out of it or not. But there's only one way to find out where it will take you: by entering it. The rest is up to you.'

Rahman turned his head and looked at Javid. Then he stared into the darkness of the void. He took a deep breath, then entered.

Notes

1. Javid-Naman – literally 'those whose names will live on forever' – is the collective name given to protestors and others allegedly killed by the Iranian regime's forces.
2. Bloody Friday, also known as the Zahedan massacre (30 September 2022), was a series of violent crackdowns by security forces in response to protests in the city of Zahedan. The protests were sparked by the alleged rape of a 15-year-old girl by a police colonel and the death of Mahsa Amini on 16 September 2022, which had already provoked widespread protests and revolt across the country against the Islamic regime. The government's crackdown in Zahedan resulted in the deaths of at least 96 protestors and left 300 injured.
3. Mohandes means 'engineer', but is used as a formal term of address, recognising his perceived technical expertise.
4. The Baloch people are a nomadic ethnic group native to the Balochistan region, which extends across Iran, Afghanistan, and Pakistan. They constitute the largest ethnic demographic in Sistan and Baluchestan, one of the driest provinces in Iran.
5. 'Haji' is used as a respectful term of address, as well as the more formal 'Haj Aqa.'

The Milkman of Xi Jinping Town

Behzad Ghadimi

Translated by Susan Niazi

THE SUNSET WAS BATHING the tumbledown cells of Kourehrash market with red light. The place teemed with people and a fetid smell of chickens' and crows' feet assailed Sadiq's nostrils. He was scared. The whole thing was terrifying. They say at night, you could be beheaded in this market and no one would hear you cry. It was getting dark. Sadiq reached into his underwear and felt the leather bag fastened under his crotch. There, he had hidden all the money he and his friend Mohammadreza had left. His testicles were frozen and shrunken. Breathing out a sigh, he started to make his way apprehensively towards the Kurdish corner. Being so tall, Sadiq always stood out. His prominent temples and bony cheeks gave him the appearance of an animated skeleton. He was an easy target and he knew it. But there was nothing he could do so he carried a switchblade up his sleeve in case of trouble. He knew, of course, that it would take more than a switchblade to keep him alive in this strange neighbourhood. He was meeting with Shaban, a Kurdish smuggler who he'd gone to great trouble to find. Shaban had promised to bring him a brass ball–valve, and had told Sadiq to wait for him at the Kurdish corner of the Kourehrash market early in the evening until he came to complete the deal. He'd already taken half of Sadiq's money as a deposit. So if he failed to show up, Sadiq and Mohammadreza would be facing ruin. Sadiq was restless. His stomach churned. Half an hour had already passed and it was almost dark. At some point he noticed a hunchbacked old man watching him discreetly from his market cell.

'Lad,' he whispered, 'what're you looking for?'

Sadiq gulped: 'Brass…'

The old man raised his eyebrows: 'Brass is for rich folk.[1] Got loads of money, have ya? Nobody sells brass around here.'

'No… My friend was going to bring me a brass knife.'

'A brass knife! You should've said so to begin with! Com'ere, I've got two or three good ones. Come and see if any of them suits you. How much money have ya got?'

'I've already paid for it,' Sadiq replied anxiously. 'I've got no money left. I'm just waiting for my guy to bring it.'

The old man gave a mocking laugh and sneered: 'Which village did you come from, lad? You've already paid for a knife, and yet you're still waiting for the guy to bring it to ya? Not very bright that! He's eaten your money and swallowed it down with a glass of water!'

'No, he will. He promised he'd bring it…'

'Yeah, and you'll be stuck waiting here for the grass to grow under your feet! Go home, lad; he's already got your money. You're just wasting your time here.'

Sadiq swallowed again. He was about to say something back when suddenly a hoarse, harsh voice interrupted them:

'Hey, Yaghoub! Are ya trying to steal my customer, old man?'

Sadiq turned and saw the brawny figure of Shaban dressed in black behind him. Shaban sported a bushy handlebar moustache and wore a worn-out *kolah makhmali*[2] on his head. The old man broke into a cold sweat and fear clouded his eyes.

'Shaboon Khan,[3] my mistake,' he grovelled. 'I didn't know he was your customer. I thought someone else had ripped off the poor boy.'

'Mind your damn business, hunchback,' Shaban growled. 'And shut the hell up.'

He turned to Sadiq and whispered in his ear: 'Did ya get the money?'

Sadiq unconsciously covered his crotch. His throat felt dry.

'First the ball-valve!' he said.

Shaban snickered, grabbing Sadiq's skinny wrist, pulling him along:

'Can't give it to ya here. You got the money or not?'

Sadiq was silent. He couldn't open his mouth. Shaban turned back and glared threateningly into his timid eyes. It was rumoured Shaban had murdered his business partner and buried his remains in his cellar. Shaban's glower burned into Sadiq's brain.

'I'll cut yer head off right now if you've got no money,' he muttered, 'you waste of skin.'

You could see Sadiq's fear by the pulse of the veins in his temples. If he lost the money now there would be no choice for him, and Mohammadreza, but to bring Mohammadreza's divorced mother, Mehri, with them to the market. If they ran out of options, her body might be the commodity they could trade.

Sadiq loved Mehri, but it was a well-kept secret. His secret love for her forced him into taking such risks with Mohammadreza. As these thoughts crossed Sadiq's mind, he girded himself, and impulsively shook his free hand. The switchblade slipped down into his left hand. He tempered his voice and said forcefully: 'Shaboon Khan! I've got nothing to lose. I just want the ball-valve. That's what I came for. First the ball-valve, then your money.'

Shaban smiled crookedly and said in his rough voice: 'Aha, I like that. You're serious. OK, no problem. Shaking down a customer isn't to my taste anyway. C'mon, follow me.'

Shaban dropped Sadiq's wrist and threaded his way quickly through the skinny, sweaty people in the market. Sadiq chased after Shaban, trying not to lose him. Reaching the end of a secondary alley, Shaban pulled out a key and opened a small cell door. He struck a match and lit an oil lamp. The dim light barely brightened the narrow space of the cell. Shaban stepped behind an old wooden table and took out a package wrapped in cloth.

'Shut the door, boy,' he said emphatically.

Sadiq closed the door cautiously behind him. Shaban unwrapped the cloth. At that moment, Sadiq saw it, shining under the dim glow from the oil lamp: the ball-valve.

'There it is!' Shaban grunted. 'A twenty-bar pressure brass ball-valve. Brand new. See this written here, made in October 2053. In other words, it was made exactly two months ago. How's that?'

The year 2053 had been a disastrous year for Sadiq. It was a year of famine, hunger and cholera which included the death of Reza, Mohammadreza's father, the only person in their town whose business – a modest little dairy store – seemed to survive. Sadiq worked at the store, but now with Mohammadreza's father gone, the store fell into trouble too. Mohammadreza and Sadiq struggled to keep the store operating. The price of milk became more expensive each day, and people stopped buying yogurt and cheese. Three months after Reza's death, the diary store went belly up. He felt like a failure. Shaban's voice brought Sadiq back to the present:

'Where's the rest of my money?'

Sadiq looked at the year 2053 inscribed on the ball-valve hesitantly. 'Does it work?' he asked. 'Is it any good, Shaboon Khan?'

'Do you doubt me, boy?'

'No I don't,' Sadiq replied.

'Show me your money before you piss me off, sonny.'

Sadiq gulped. The ball-valve looked new. Faucets and plumbing fixtures were not available just anywhere. If the security forces of the Petrogaz Company caught anyone with such things, they would have them killed on the spot. The only thing they killed people over was the huge, high-pressure oil pipes that traversed the country, taking oil from the south of Iran to the border. Being in possession of a ball-valve meant only one thing: you were stealing it from the Petrogaz Company.

'C'mon boy!' Shaban yelled. 'The money?'

'Need to find a bathroom first,' Sadiq mumbled awkwardly.

'You wanna piss? Later! You gotta give me my money now.'

'The money is in...' Sadiq paused, then continued: 'In my pants.'

Shaban looked surprised for a moment, then suddenly burst out laughing.

'Go!' he said, clapping his hands. 'The washroom is behind the cell. If ya get any shit on my money, I'll cut your head off.'

'Don't worry, it's clean. It's in a bag.'

'C'mon, you sneaky little asshole.'

Five minutes later, Shaban was counting Sadiq's money. Sadiq reached for the ball-valve which was on the table, but Shaban put his hand on it.

'Where ya stealing oil from, lad?' he asked.

Sadiq went pale. 'We're not stealing oil,' he snapped.

'Bullshit kid, a brass ball-valve with twenty-bar pressure can only be used for one thing: oil theft... Where's the hole?'

Sadiq wouldn't answer. Mohammadreza had told him if he revealed their location for the heist, their work would all be for nothing.

'Shaboon Khan,' he stammered, 'I swear on the Quran, I've got no idea. I'm taking the ball-valve for my boss. I don't know what he wants to do with it. I just know if I don't get it to him, or if it's broken, or I lose it, or whatever, he'll cut my mum's head off. That's all.'

Shaban looked insultingly into young Sadiq's bony face.

'Who's your boss?' he asked.

Sadiq knew that he would have to give him a name to avoid further questioning. So he offered the most notorious name in Xi Jinping Town.

'Ramazoon, the Ice Seller,' he said. 'He's our boss.'

Shaban pondered this. He took his hand off the ball-valve and said: 'Ok, I'll talk to Ramazoon myself about this later.'

Sadiq hurriedly wrapped the ball-valve in the cloth and stuck it under his shabby coat. He didn't even remember whether he said goodbye. He just hit the alley and ran to the wagons terminal of Xi Jinping Town.

He had lied to Shaban, of course. Sadiq and Mohammadreza didn't steal oil for Ramazoon, the Ice Seller. They stole for themselves. When Reza, Mohammadreza's father, lay dying, he revealed a long-kept secret to his son: the location of a hidden junction point that he installed into the Petrogaz pipeline. Mohammadreza's father had worked for the multinational company in his early days. It was in the year 2033 when the Strait of Hormoz had gone dry and the oil tankers were unable to sail through carrying Iranian oil anymore. It was then that the Petrogaz Company started to build huge pipelines; a scheme that saw the company give food and weapons to the government in return for freshly-piped Iranian oil. Reza had told Mohammadreza that when they were working on the pipelines, he'd added a hidden junction point in the pipelines; somewhere beneath the huge tangle of pipes, crossing the Urmia Swamp.[4] The problem was that the ball-valve connected to the junction branch for stealing had become faulty. Mohammadreza had told Sadiq all about this and how he was unable to steal oil from the pipe any longer. He confided that the dairy store had never provided enough for them to live off on its own; stolen oil was the only thing that guaranteed income in that little store. Their plan was to replace the junction point's ball-valve and siphon the oil into a jerrycan. They could then hide the jerrycan under the milk they were selling. When it was safe, they would take the oil to an illegal gasoline workshop in the city of Zanjan. There, according to Mohammadreza, they could sell the oil at a profit. They called the workshop 'The Refinery' although the whole thing was cobbled together from dismantled car-engine pipes and a broken oven. It distilled oil and produced mostly diesel and a little gasoline. Gasoline was particularly expensive. Those who still had money ran their engines and generators on diesel mostly, rather than the gasoline they were designed to use. Gasoline was a luxury product for only the wealthiest customers.

Until a week ago, Sadiq knew nothing about all these strange goings-on. He thought he was working in a simple dairy store. Now that Reza was dead, he had hoped he might somehow get closer to Mehri, Mohammadreza's mother. He was thinking of Mehri's ample breasts and her firm ass. A woman who seemed ageless; so young and beautiful. He had no idea how he could express his affections to Mehri, all he knew was Mohammadreza's warning: if they weren't stealing oil within two weeks, he would have to send her to work at Khodarooh's brothel. It was true. There were no other choices left. Khodarooh had already offered them good money for Mehri, but he would only send her to serve the foreign employees of the Petrogaz Company. Sadiq couldn't tolerate it. He would rather die rather than see this happen. That was the reason why, three nights ago, he shook hands with Mohammadreza and swore that, together, they would replace the junction point's ball-valve, no matter what. They were risking death and they both knew it. But there was no choice.

As Sadiq sat in the Xi Jinping Town wagon, he calmly put his hand on his stomach where he had hidden the ball-valve in the cloth under his coat. A little spark of hope flickered in his heart. If they replaced the ball-valve, if they siphoned the oil into the jerrycan, if they hid the jerrycan with milk on top of it, if they took the oil to Zanjan and sold it to the refinery, then everything would be better. Then things would be fine. Sadiq bore a faint smile on his bony face. He allowed himself to daydream for a moment until the harsh voice of the wagon driver woke him up; they had reached the town.

Xi Jinping Town was the name given to the newly established city. The Chinese president had built it on the ruins of the old, abandoned village of Kahriz, mainly to accommodate Petrogaz employees. It was a town built on a 'mechanical design' approach, inspired by Greater Shanghai but not as large and as ordered as that city. The locals couldn't afford to buy or rent anywhere inside the town, so instead they built shacks on the outskirts. They were able to make a bit of money in Xi Jinping Town, often selling low-quality food. The main sources of money, of course, came from selling drugs and prostitution. No one cared about the locals. Prostitution and drugs increased the productivity of the Petrogaz workers and made them want to stay longer, reducing their desire to return to their own homes in their native countries which were still green and lush with water. Here was a lawless frontier, where they could live without consequence.

Every morning, the sanitary workers from the town collected the dead bodies of prostitutes and locals and took them away to be burned or used for some other purpose which no one ever knew about...

Sadiq didn't pay any mind to such thoughts when he finally arrived at Mohammadreza's door. The stench of sour yogurt and old grease didn't disgust him either as he had grown up with such smells. Mohammadreza was sitting on a box at the entrance to the store, rolling a cigarette. Seeing Mohammadreza's profile outside the place reassured Sadiq and restored his strength and purpose.

'I've got it, it's with me,' Sadiq said, as he approached.

'Now what?'

'There's my man,' Mohammadreza beamed. 'I knew I could count on you.'

'Always, mate.'

Sadiq handed the ball-valve to Mohammadreza, who stuck the freshly rolled cigarette into Sadiq's mouth, then held out a light for it, before turning to check over the ball-valve. He was satisfied. Very satisfied. His face became flushed. Excited, Sadiq sucked hard and fast on the cigarette. Mohammadreza popped quickly into the dairy store. Five minutes later he was out with a backpack: 'Let's go.'

'Right now?' Sadiq asked.

'When would you like us to go?' Mohammadreza teased. 'You aren't chickening out, are you?'

'Mamreza! If they find the ball-valve on us, they'll kill us on the spot.'

'That's why we can't waste any time.' Mohammadreza pounced. 'The longer we take, the better the chance that some snitch will rat us out. We get the ball-valve installed now and nobody will know any different.'

Sadiq felt a sharp pain in his head. He weighed their odds. He didn't have anyone special in his life so nobody would ever miss him, but he wasn't sure he was ready to die either. His hands became sweaty.

'We made a pact!' Mohammadreza snapped at him. 'Don't back out now.'

'I'm not backing out,' Sadiq replied.

'So you scared?'

Sadiq didn't answer.

Mohammadreza answered for him: 'I'm scared too, but we've got no choice, Sadiq. You know it. We'll figure it out. It'll be ok. Don't be scared.'

'How're we gonna get there?' Sadiq asked.

'Donkey!' Mohammadreza declared.

'You're the donkey,' Sadiq muttered.

'No, I meant we'll go by donkey,' Mohammadreza explained.

'You've never had a donkey. Who did you get it from?'

'What's the name of that Asian guy at the end of the alley? The one whose name is hard to pronounce,' Mohammadreza asked.

'Oh him? I think it's Xiahui,' Sadiq offered.

'I rented it from him,' Mohammadreza explained. 'I told him I had to take milk to Tabriz.'

'I'm not prepared,' Sadiq sputtered. 'Have you got the tools ready? Water and food?'

'I put everything in the donkey's saddlebag,' Mohammadreza reassured him. 'Look, if we leave now, we'll be there around two or three in the morning. That's the best time. C'mon, Sadiq, I can't do it by myself.'

'You're afraid to go alone – is that it?' Sadiq snapped. 'But I already went by myself to get the ball-valve, didn't I?'

Mohamamdreza flushed, frowned, and pursed his lips. He reached out and took the cigarette from Sadiq. Taking a deep drag on it, he looked down the alley, blowing out the lungful of smoke as he did so. 'I'm scared,' he began. 'You got more guts than me. You've always had more guts than me. But that doesn't mean I'm a chicken. Ok, I admit: you've got more guts than me. So are we going to go now or what?'

'OK let's go,' Sadiq said, slapping him on the back. 'We'll do it now and get it over with. It'll either work or it won't. Whatever happens is better than the shit we're in now.'

So they left. In the dark, they used a kerosene lantern to light the dim path down a rutted and well-travelled road, taking Xiahui's donkey with them. They each took turns riding the beast while the other strode alongside. The roadside was littered with the rusted metal hulks of abandoned scrapped cars. They could see tall concrete spikes sticking out of the ground along the roadside, dangling long strands of wires that resembled weeping willow branches. According to

Mohammadreza, in the time before this age of cholera and famine, lights and electricity were believed to have hummed along these wires. Now the strands hung uselessly where they had been cut and stolen as high as hands and ladders could reach, leaving the rest to dangle from the concrete spikes.

They sneaked past the Company's patrols, and stealthily bypassed the shacks built by nomadic thieves. They had learnt how to do such things in childhood and knew, all too well, how to survive in the chaotic remnants of that once-great civilisation, and how to avoid trouble. They knew how to hide and how to escape; how to pilfer and extort from those weaker than them; how to pay off the bullies; how to kowtow to their superiors and prey on those inferior. It was the kind of knowledge that was crucial for Sadiq and Mohammadreza's survival in these harsh times.

The howling of the dogs had already gone silent for an hour or so when Sadiq and Mohammadreza waded up to their knees in the mud of Urmia. They could see the huge round oil pipelines criss-crossing the wetlands.

'From here on, it gets dangerous,' Mohammadreza warned, dimming the light. 'We've got to grope our way along in the darkness. Tie the donkey behind that abandoned bus over there.' After a short pause, he hissed: 'No, tie it *inside* the bus. Give it a Valium to make it sleep.'

'Did you bring Valium?' Sadiq asked.

Mohammadreza reached into the donkey's saddlebag and pulled out a small bottle. He took out three pills and gave them to Sadiq. 'Give the donkey these pills with a sugar cube so he'll swallow them.'

'Won't these kill him?' Sadiq asked.

'With three Chinese Valiums?' Mohammadreza scoffed. 'He won't die. I just hope they're enough. If he lets out a bray, we'll be done for in this mud.'

Mohammadreza took the ball-valve from the saddlebag and grabbed the tool box. Sadiq took the donkey onto the dilapidated bus which was stranded in the mud. A quarter of an hour later, lugging a twenty-litre jerrycan and a dimmed lantern, Sadiq caught up to Mohammadreza.

'Kill the light,' Mohammadreza hissed angrily. 'If anyone sees it, they'll be on us like ants and grasshoppers.'

'Mamreza! How're we gonna find our way, man?' Sadiq beseeched him. 'Do you have any idea where we're going?'

Mohammadreza wiped his sweaty forehead with his sleeve, and swallowed. 'I know where,' he said in a firm voice. 'From here on, follow me. Dad told me what to look for and what signs to use to find my way. We'll know where from the number of steps after the pipes' turn.'

'What turn?'

Mohammadreza pointed to the place where a huge cluster of pipes coming from the east abruptly turned towards the north, like a Leviathan changing course in the middle of the Urmia swamp. Killing the light completely, taking off their shoes, and rolling up their trouser legs, the oil thieves took to the swamp.

Into the darkness, Mohammadreza followed the step-by-step directions his father had given him, like a hound following a scent, with Sadiq following him nervously through the mire. The swamp became deeper. Soon they were up to their chests. Mohammadreza stopped. Then he turned his head. There was a look of relief in his eyes.

'It should be down here,' he whispered.

'Mamreza! It's getting too deep, man,' Sadiq pleaded. 'We're sinking here. We'll drown if we're not careful.'

'No. Step in my footsteps,' his friend intoned.

'What kind of place is this?'

'If it were easy to get to, they'd have found it long ago, Sadiq. My father deliberately put the junction point in the shittiest place to find.'

'We're sitting ducks if anyone sees us, man. We can't move in this state.'

'Don't jinx us,' Mohammadreza chided. 'C'mon.'

They were almost up to their necks in the mire, following the pipes, when Mohammadreza suddenly ducked under them. Sadiq couldn't make out the junction point he was heading for. 'Where is this goddamn point?' he asked anxiously.

'It should be somewhere right around here.'

But neither of them could see it. 'Let me light the lamp,' Sadiq suggested. 'We can't find it like this.'

'No, don't,' Mohammadreza snapped.

'We aren't gonna find it otherwise,' Sadiq replied. 'I'll cover it with my hands. I'll hold it up between the pipes before I light it. It won't be visible.'

Mohammadreza lowered his head.

'Hope you brought us to the right spot,' Sadiq added. 'If you've screwed up, I'll bury you right here.'

'It should be right here,' Mohammadreza insisted. 'We followed all of my father's instructions to the letter. It must be here somewhere.'

Holding the oil lamp up between the pipes, Sadiq took a match and lit it, keeping it as its lowest flame. There it was: a tiny pipe that was hanging down from one of the giant ones, dangling like the penis of a dying old man. There were tears in Sadiq's eyes.

'There, do you see it!' Mohammadreza said loudly, no longer able to whisper. 'See, it's exactly where I said! This is it! My father's junction. Can't you see I was right?'

Sadiq hugged his friend and simultaneously covered his mouth. 'Don't yell Mamreza, for God's sake,' he whispered. 'Way to go! But stop yelling. Right on to your dad too! Let's change the goddamn ball-valve and collect some oil.'

'Look, it has two control valves,' Mohammadreza said breathlessly. 'God knows how much pressure is in these pipes. We have to be very careful. We have to close the first control valve completely, and then change the ball-valve.'

Sadiq nodded, and crossed his hands to boost Mohammadreza up, so he could clamber silently up onto the pipes above them. Once up, he straddled one of them and started asking for specific types of wrenches, whispering their names, for Sadiq to pass up. It took him half an hour to change the ball-valve. When Mohammadreza dropped the old ball-valve down to Sadiq, he could see how worn and scratched it was.

'What happened? Have you replaced it? Is it gonna work?' Sadiq asked hesitantly.

'I don't know. Pass me up the can.'

Mohammadreza turned the tap, and at the smell of the oil, Sadiq felt briefly intoxicated. As he heard the oil gushing into the jerrycan, he closed his eyes. It was the most beautiful sound he had ever heard. Half an hour later, they were picking their way back to where they started. The path was the same, but this time they didn't feel tired or afraid; they didn't walk so much as danced. They started laughing for no reason. They were about a hundred paces from the bus when Mohammadreza said, 'Wait a minute.'

'What's wrong?'

'Look. Put the can down for a minute.'

Sadiq set the can down carefully on the mud.

Mohammadreza took a breath and looked at the sky. 'You're not supposed to know the location of the junction,' he said. 'This is the only legacy my father left me. Without it, my mother would have to work for Khodarooh.'

'What do you mean?'

'Nothing,' he said. 'Except that this is where we say goodbye.'

An ominous feeling crept into Sadiq's heart. He saw that Mohammadreza had taken something from behind his back. It was a pistol.

'What're you doing?' Sadiq groaned. 'I'm supposed to be your friend.'

'You're not my friend. You think I don't know what you think about my mother, you bastard?'

Sadiq's voice choked in his throat. Before he could do anything, Mohammadreza pulled the trigger. The bullet hit Sadiq in his left shoulder, exploding pain through his body. Without thinking, he dove into the marsh water. Another shot sounded but this one didn't hit. There was mud in his ears and mouth. The fear of death electrified him. Suddenly the sound of machine guns was heard. Sadiq heard a moan and then a thud. He didn't know what was happening. Slowly, he moved his hands and feet and pulled himself gingerly through the swamp. He kept himself hidden in the marsh water at all times. Suddenly it was as bright as day. An intense beam of light played over the spot where Mohammadreza had shot Sadiq a few minutes earlier. The machine guns fired again. Sadiq couldn't tell where the bullets were coming from. They were being sprayed back and forth over the surface of the lake. Mohammadreza's body had burst like a bloody balloon and began to disintegrate under the heavy gunfire. Sadiq held his breath in fear. Without thinking, he pushed himself further and further into the swamp, away from the disaster.

The shooting stopped. His shoulder was broken and bleeding. The spotlight was turned off. Sadiq crawled as fast as he could to reach the shore. He hurt all over. His temples throbbed. He stumbled towards the wreckage of the bus and as he reached Xiaohui's donkey, he heard the sound of the Petrogaz Company's helicopter, slapping the sky with its rotors. Sadiq tried to wake the donkey up, but the donkey was sleeping as soundly as the dead. Not knowing what to do, he started to run. He ran with every last ounce of energy he had. He didn't ever look back.

★

The summer of 2054 was even worse than the year before. Famine and cholera were widespread, but not for Sadiq. He had just returned from his trip to Zanjan and things were looking good for him as he knocked on the fibreglass door of Khodarouh's house. A few minutes later, the old man's gruff voice was heard: 'Who is it?'

'Khodarouh Khan! It's me, Sadiq.'

The old man opened the door. His long beard was sparse and patchy. His eyebrows stuck out like a horned owl; he had an awkward face. His mouth twisted, it was the closest gesture he could muster to resemble a laugh. He welcomed Sadiq and motioned him in.

'You came to see Mehri, didn't you?' he said teasingly.

Sadiq blushed but didn't say anything. Mehri was now working for Khodarouh. The poor woman who had lost both her husband and son had had no other choice. Sadiq's shy steps led him into a small back room tucked away behind a dirty red curtain as if it was hiding from the rest of the house.

'Mehri Khanoom,'[5] Sadiq called from behind the curtain, 'it's me.'

Khodarouh Khan blew a raspberry and shouted: 'Stop goofing around. Get your clothes off and get in there. She has another customer in half an hour. Get in there and finish your business!'

Sadiq pulled aside the curtain and entered. Mehri was lying lifelessly on the mattress with her bare breasts exposed. She was delirious. It was clear that she had just injected something. Sadiq's eyes brimmed with tears. He knelt down in front of her. Her eyes were vacant, she wasn't seeing anything.

'Don't beat me!' she slurred. 'Beating me will cost you double.'

Sadiq gagged. He looked away and wiped his tears. He took out a small package from his coat and stuffed it into Mehri's hand. He whispered into Mehri's ear:

'Mehri Jan, this is money. Keep it somewhere where that old hyena won't find it. I'll be back again with more for you. Keep hanging on. I'll get you out of here.'

Mehri's eyes were blinking sightlessly.

'Do you want it from behind?' she mumbled. Sadiq stared at her for a long time. Then, as if from nowhere, a flicker of recognition danced across Mehri's face. 'Get out!' she screamed. 'Get out! You are the cause of all this! It should have been you who died! Get out!'

Sadiq stumbled backwards, eventually finding his feet and running.

In the courtyard, Khodarouh was sitting on an empty pail by the door. 'That was fast!' he said in a hoarse voice.

Then he burst into laughter, exposing his rotted teeth, it was as if his whole body had been rotten and dead for a long time.

'How much do I owe you?' Sadiq asked.

The old man gave a number, and Sadiq thrust a few bills into the wrinkled hands of the pimp of Xi Jinping Town. He was about to leave when Khodarouh grabbed his wrist: 'Stop boy!'

'What?'

'Don't fall in love with Mehri!' he croaked.

'Sure,' Sadiq answered. 'Why are you telling me this?'

'Mehri is not one of mine anymore,' the old man explained, 'nor anyone else's. One of the Company's managers took a liking to her and he'll be coming round one of these days to take her away.'

Sadiq's hands began to tremble. 'I'm telling you, don't do anything foolish,' the filthy old man whispered. 'The guy's some big, top-brass thick-neck. He'll ruin yours, mine and everyone's life and business.'

Sadiq couldn't stand it anymore. His shoulders started to shake. Khodarouh patted him on the back.

'Pull yourself together, man,' he said. 'Mehri couldn't have ever been a bride for you.'

Sadiq was crying silently.

'Come and enjoy her a final time,' Khodarouh said in a

softer voice. 'Before the guy takes her away. After that, God knows if you'll ever see her again.'

Notes

1. In Farsi, the word for 'brass' has the same pronunciation and spelling as the word for 'rice'. Rice is an expensive food just as brass is an expensive metal, so the idiom works on both readings.
2. *Kolah Makhmali* refers to a type of black, velvet fedora hat. In Iranian culture, it denotes a social group of men who call themselves '*luṭi's* (tough guys). According to the Encyclopaedia Iranica: 'in the 19th and 20th centuries *luṭis* were often referred to as 'roughs' (*owbāš*), 'knife-wielders' (*chāqu-kešān*), or 'thick-necks' (*gardan-e koloft*) and were used to organise 'spontaneous' demonstrations, even participating in opposing demonstrations on consecutive days. The most famous example was the demonstration led by Ša'bān-e Bimoḵ that toppled Prime Minister Mosaddagh in 1953.'
3. Khan is a term of respect which follows the name of a man.
4. This references Lake Urmia, which is still a lake today, but is beginning to dry up due to poor environmental practices.
5. 'Khanoom' is a term of respect which follows the name of a woman.

Due Date

Mohammad Tolouei

Translated by Farzaneh Doosti

I AM LEANING ON the edge of the terrace, crunching scraps of bread from the night before and spreading them on the black granite parapet. This is really just my excuse to peep into the prison yard every day – to peep into a corner where the prisoners are strolling, or rather to contemplate those orderly, moving masses down there as the bodies of fighters who keep the fire of the revolution burning in our hearts. I cherish this hope – that there comes a day when we can decide for ourselves how we want to live. Erfan's voice is heard from inside the house: he's left a lengthy message propounding my father's quarrel with Firouzeh again. I want to tell him it's none of our business – neither mine nor his – but I can't do it. I can't just say such words to my half-brother; it may seem like I am siding with my father – which is the last thing I want. I throw all the stuff I need into a bag and place it at the door. I have to fetch an emergency light, as it is getting overcast, and we are likely to stay in total darkness. I am scared of being in the dark. Once, I stepped inside Israfil's protective case and the door locked behind me, or maybe I closed the door myself. I was just seven years old, but I've been afraid of the dark ever since.

'Find a battery too,' I tell Israfil, 'but you should swallow it. I don't dare carry it with me.'

Who would dare carry a power bank nowadays, given that we have to wait at every zone's checkpoint. Sooner or later the officers would get suspicious of the way we drag our heels, and they'd come and search the pedaluxe.

'You can drink some phosphorescence,' I tell Israfil, 'so you can glow when it gets dark.'

'My skin is not capable of allowing light to radiate through it,' Israfil says.

He never gets my sense of humour. A programmer somewhere must have written a plug-in for these old Ramas to allow them to understand the multifaceted nature of words, but it's never readily available and I've never found it when I've needed it. 'You really can't find a second-hand X14 interface?' I ask him.

When I was twelve, I once asked my father's Rama what his name was on his own planet. But he had never seen his own planet, he told me; he had been cloned on earth. We called it Israfil[1] because my father told it to turn on Radio Health every morning, and turn the volume up to wake us. *It is recommended that you keep 1.8-metre distance from the others to stay sound and safe. Take your immunity-boosters every day. Never go out in public without your collagen skin.*

Israfil simultaneously repeated the radio host's words along with her, in a sweet bass voice my father had selected. Israfil was one of the antique E.R.C. models with a protective case and GPS that had been smuggled on a mule across the mountains of Iraqi Kurdistan. It had neither on/off buttons, nor a colour screen, nor audio bands, nor 360-degree eyesight.

Israfil looks exactly like what the first Ramas looked like when they first set foot on the earth with their oversized heads and frail, seven-fingered hands, more reminiscent of images of starving refugees from the last century than aliens from space.

I always know how Israfil will respond, still I type 'X14

connector' into my searchband, out of habit. The first page shows repetitive information. I unwrap my searchband from my wrist and put it on the table. We all need to keep our searchbands within a safe distance from ourselves. Safe means near enough to detect our vital signals. They say searchbands and Ramas are interconnected and exchange data but nobody knows how they do this. We read about such things in the letters the prisoners write – that the government is controlling us and to resist, we have to disconnect from the Ramas. But their words make no logical sense. Even that group of crazies that moved out into the Semnan Deserts, to live like primitives without any energy-consuming devices... *even they* have taken their Ramas with them!

Today I need to find a goldsmith in the bazaar who can make a C-shaped X connector, and not charge me an arm and a leg for it. Without such a calibrated piece, I can't use anything in the house. Without the golden C, all the energy-using devices in the house stopped working. Super chargers control every aspect of our lives and the government controls the super chargers. In this way, we are captives, no different from the prisoners in the jail across the street. Like all those ones who see the world through a narrow slit. The prison opposite our complex has been there for years. Each new government has promised to demolish it, but ended up just leaving it to itself. Evin Prison is the only place in the city that still bears its old name and still retains a few square metres of fertile land on which things grow. Every spring, everyone sits on their terraces at Atisaz Complex and stares at the crows strolling around the prison hill and picking at the meadow. In summer, the grass on the hill catches fire and soldiers run with extinguishers to put it out. It's like watching a comedy from two centuries ago where people would fall to the ground for no reason and the audiences would chortle, also for no reason. In winter, no one bothers with watching the crows prowling over the snow. Everyone has a loved one imprisoned in one of those cells. Some people even do things on purpose to be taken in there so that they can survive the winter cold. They swallow batteries and smuggle them into the political prisoners' ward so they can send out their letters. In winter, all kinds of people end up in the prison, from the hungry to businessmen to political activists, but winters are so hard on people that no one remembers them. Not even a single photo of them can be found in the searchbands' memories. Winter is a time for forgetting.

The bread scraps I have spread over the edge draw the crows more than sparrows or doves. I walk towards the crows and make noises but they won't go. Israfil is playing some Russian musical epic, one of those pieces of music with tenors and sopranos singing at the top of their range. He says it's the soundtrack to a film about Alexander Nevsky, but no information can be found on the searchband, as if it's been erased everywhere, except for in Israfil's memory. When did I last go to the bazaar? Long before the new zoning and curfew laws came into force, for sure, so that's definitely more than twelve years ago. What did I do the last time I went to the bazaar? Shamim must have been with me. She was the one who always showed me around it – the restaurants, the old chambers, she even took me to a store in the shoemakers' market, where she pulled up a hatch, and showed me the running water of an old qanat. I asked Israfil to look around and see where I had left the pedaluxe. Without thinking, he said, 'In Parking Lot Minus 2.'

After the National Stored Energy Prohibition Law was passed, no vehicle that used stored energy was allowed on the roads. You can take a pedaluxe out, because it doesn't even use a solar-powered battery, but it's not always certain it won't be confiscated. Such matters have long been arbitrarily interpreted. Sometimes, the zone preservation committees start to fight with each other, and then what might be a normal act in one zone can be called a crime in another. I wrap my searchband round my wrist. It grips hard against my skin, tightening; it's checking my pulse and blood pressure, but it's not clear where this data is being transmitted to. Having a searchband is compulsory. Previously, only the extremely wealthy, drug-dealers, and professional athletes had one, but after the pandemic it became mandatory.

'Why don't Ramas leave people alone to live their lives?' I ask Israfil.

His eyes widen, alarmed by the idea of being abandoned and that I might even consider it. 'Ramas don't know how to leave,' he says.

'Perhaps it's time they learnt such things from people after all these years,' I say.

I always talk politely and cautiously with Israfil. I always assume he knows things about me that I'd rather no one else knew, and that if I upset him unintentionally, he might go and share these secrets or innermost thoughts with a friend or enemy, and that friend or enemy might see me on the street one day and say: 'Farzam! When you were nine years old, you peed in your pants on a bus from Tehran to Yazd, because the girl in the next seat was watching you and you didn't want to go and pee in the desert while she stared down at you.' It's true, of course. I did indeed pee my pants because a girl was watching me. Is this such an unspeakable secret?

'Have you ever wanted to talk about me to anyone else?' I ask Israfil.

'To whom?' he asks.

'To anyone. To my father, to Firouzeh, to Erfan?'

'Why do you think they matter to me? I'm your Rama.'

'If you're my Rama,' I say, 'why can't you just find me a connector?'

Israfil slides open the aluminium door and steps out onto the balcony and stands there, barely peeking over the parapet. He turns the music off, and tries to communicate with another Rama and, through him, with all other living Ramas on the planet. 'I've found a place that makes them,' he says. 'But do you really want to go?'

'We'll be left in the dark if we don't.' I say.

Being left in the dark is the worst thing you can threaten someone with nowadays. We enter the lift. Israfil's head barely reaches my chest as he faces me, avoiding his own reflection in the mirror.

'Do you call yourselves 'Ramas' among yourselves?' I ask.

It takes a while for him to contemplate this, but the expression on his face resembles my father's contemplative look. He is my Rama and yet he wears my father's expressions, because my father was the first man he ever saw in this world. He was the first person he ever saw frown, laugh, or look surprised.

'We don't talk,' he says. 'You know this.'

'OK, what do you call each other in that mental communion?'

Israfil is not much into abstract ideas. He isn't good at examining himself or the reason for his existence, but there have been Ramas that have committed suicide and thrown themselves under a train. Israfil pretends to help me push the pedaluxe forward. Ramas can barely do anything practical with their small, delicate hands; Israfil only knows how to make gestures with them.

'Are you sure this goldsmith is still operating?' I ask. 'They haven't arrested him yet?'

Israfil shrugs, to indicate he doesn't know, but it's a meaningless gesture given how little his shoulders budge. No microorganism can survive on a Rama's skin, so it is not compulsory for them to wear collagen shells. Nevertheless, many people keep them wrapped in shells just for good measure. Some people hang copper collars on their shelled Ramas or put scary masks over their faces; others inject volume-boosting biochemical bulking agents into their muscles to make them look more imposing, but everyone knows never to expect any trouble from a Rama. Ramas prefer to contemplate upon the world, and would only dare steal food from hamsters.

As we make our way to the Zone Seven gates, we don't say a word. It's natural for people under collagen shells not to talk. The voice is weakened by the shells and you have to constantly repeat yourself. Some people believe it's a symptom of depression and conduct pointless research into the subject, and somehow get funding for it. As we ride along the Modarres Highway, we notice gaps between trees on either side are filled with luminous silicon branches that absorb ultraviolet light. We move very slowly, slower than a cyclist, because pedaluxes have a heavy trunk and it's only me pedalling, me and a Rama whose leg muscles are no good for anything.

At the gate, they keep us waiting. They make you wait every time until, who knows, maybe someone will come along and unleash a barrage on us, or throw an incendiary grenade at us. It's always like this. They make you wait until it gets dark so they can charge you with a night-time admission fee, or until you get so stressed you're willing to bribe them to get through.

'See if there's anyone here from the mean streets of Atisaz, in Zone Seven,' I tell Israfil.

After thinking for moment, he says, 'No.'

A Rama's answers are always like this: precise. They never mix emotion with information. They don't make concessions to emotions or exaggerate the significance of anything. They simply tell you without any hesitation if something is the case or not.

'And no one wants to accompany us?' I say.

I should have asked these questions before we set off, but I was too busy thinking about the dark nights ahead, and the government repairman who laughed when he arrived and took one glance at the X14 connector, saying he'd changed three chargers on his way to this block. There had been an audible irony to his words, implying that I needed to bribe him now. 'I won't pay for something the government is responsible for,' I said.

The repairman asked for some water, then sat down on one of the high-backed chairs, whose legs had mountain ranges carved on them. The loaders were standing in a queue like worker ants waiting to carry in soil and stones.

'Why do you think you need to pay extra?' the repairman asked.

He sipped his water and waited for me to answer.

'Because we don't deserve such a living,' I said.

The representative put his glass of water on the table; on its bone-white surface, a drop had fallen. He picked up the drop with a fingertip and brought it to his mouth, then extended his tongue to lick it.

'You need to get on the waiting list. It may take you six months, even a year, to get you X14 connector.'

He stood up slowly and held out his searchband for me to sign. On his searchband's screen, my name, address and request were registered. 'Let's see when your turn comes,' he said.

I signed and a wheel started to spin on the screen, setting my turn for eleven months and twelve days from then. The agent laughed. His laugh was neither terrifying nor desperate. It just explained the situation.

'What now?' he said.

I'm not a revolutionary, but I do want to change certain things around me, very small details that could improve life a little. I do not mean the lives of all the people of my Zone, let alone everyone in Tehran, or the other city-states, or the whole globe. I only wanted to improve my life, specifically. And in that moment, I would rather have become an X14 connector smuggler, than give a single penny to that man, to a man who was making a profit out of my inaction.

'I'll find a solution,' I said.

The agent gathered his bag and tools he had spread out on

the table saying 'I could make it a bit faster for you; the only problem is the golden C-shaped head of the connector.'

It felt like watching a bad movie, a bad sci-fi film in which one man single-handedly rebels against the system, like *Soylent Green* or something. Something as stupid as someone discovering that people are being abducted and murdered and turned into biscuits, and deciding to save himself and tell the world what the system was doing to them. But my X14 connector was damaged and I couldn't play anything. Without a connecting cable, I couldn't even open the door, or run the water pumps.

As we wait in the queue in front of the gate, the temperature outside is creeping over 50 degrees Celsius. When you're in a collagen shell, that kind of heat can drive you crazy. I ask Israfil to get out of the pedaluxe. Ramas radiate heat – not much, of course, barely enough to power an Edison light bulb – but I asked him to leave anyway; perhaps he could reach out to other Ramas to see what was going on. An old hybrid car pulls up behind my pedaluxe in the queue. This is dangerous, since only government big shots and smugglers have cars nowadays, and they never need to wait in queues at Zone borders. Either the gate opens for them or they open it with force.

'Whose car is that?' I ask Israfil.

Israfil gets back in the pedaluxe, and clasps his hands to his chest. 'I guess their Ramas are isolated,' he says after a moment. 'I have no way of getting in touch with them.'

The car inches right up to us, as if wanting to stick to me, making it impossible for me to change lanes. 'Let's try a different gate, maybe one at the market,' I say. 'Something's going on here.'

Israfil shuts his eyes, and for a moment, he looks like a man brushing his teeth each morning and night, in front of the bathroom mirror, knowing that sooner or later these teeth he has been taking such a good care of will break, or fall out, or rot. There is a sort of bitterness regarding the future in the faces of all Ramas, a kind of doomed wisdom.

'Let's go to the Shemiran Gate,' I say. 'It means going through an underground highway, but it's safer than staying here like this.'

I bend and strain at the pedal, with all my force, trying to twist the pedaluxe out of its lane. The pedal turns, and the pedaluxe turns, and we head towards the underground highway. Israfil is sitting motionless, hands clasped to his chest, no longer pretending to pedal. 'You haven't spoken to your dad in a while now,' he says.

'He's busy,' I say. 'If he gets himself in trouble again, Firouzeh will call me.'

Israfil was my father's Rama, but at some point he became mine. The new Ramas need to be reset to their factory settings when they're given to a new user, but with the old models, it's more like giving away a pet. The old owner should keep their distance while the Rama gradually gets used to the new owner.

'Let's find a dealer before we reach the highway and get a battery,' I say. 'Let's not leave empty-handed.'

Israfil tried to find a Rama nearby to link with, so as to search for an active dealer in the neighbourhood of the highway. Dealers often hang out along the highway, but at the first sight of any plainclothes pretending to be customers, they shoot. In fact, sometimes they even shoot actual civilians just for looking suspicious. Dealers are very dangerous creatures; they gamble with people's lives and you have to trust them. This combination is very intimidating.

'There's one in Shabdari,' Israfil says, 'at the intersection of the third highway, but doesn't provide a link. Only sells in person.'

'Let's get a simple AC battery,' I say. 'I'm not really in the mood for the heat a solar one will bring. An AC battery only comes with a one-year prison sentence.'

We reach the third highway and are just turning the corner when we see the dealer. He is wearing a waterproof poncho over his collagen shell, and is flanked by two Ramas, covered head to toe in tattoos. One of them has the words 'I'm Tame' written on his forehead. The other has a mushroom cloud tattooed on his chest, with tiny purple flowers pouring out from its ring, along with the caption 'To the end of the world.'

Ramas' bodies are the best places for modern tattoo artists to express themselves. Likewise, small companies that don't have big marketing budgets stamp their slogans onto the bodies of Ramas, as do critical thinkers who turn their Ramas into a kind of banned book. The dealer keeps one hand hidden under the poncho – or perhaps he's missing a hand. As I approach him, I say, 'I need something to make a flashlight work again.'

I haven't bought illegal goods for a long time, and don't know which are the right words to use these days. Every time you want to buy something like this, the name changes. They used to call it Chekhus, then Penirak, and later on, Banaras. It's as if this walk of life is trying to absorb all the underused words. With his visible hand, the dealer takes out something round the size of a coin, and says, 'I possess this. But you ought to utter more clearly what suits your device.'

He's faking his accent. It's clear that he's not been to Tehran in a long time, yet he's trying to speak like a kid from Zone Five, where everyone sounds like they're mocking someone more eloquent than them.

'I can't make head nor tail out of such things,' I say. The dealer turns to the Rama with the tattoo on his forehead, and says 'See what his majesty's device is.'

His Rama and Israfil exchange glances, and his Rama slowly replies: 'A five-watt lamp, it seems.'

'Take it from them,' Israfil tells me. 'I'll fix it myself.'

A Rama's fingers are as delicate as those girls rolling Cuban cigars in black and white newsreels – they're fine enough to build watches or fashion jewellery, but only get used to scratch heads or pluck hair from knees. Ramas only do what they want to. No one can ever make them do something against their will, otherwise our factories and workshops would be full of them.

'How can I transfer the amount?' I ask the dealer.

He smiles and the smile stays on his face like the trace of a scar. 'Cash,' he says. 'We do business only in cash, sir.'

The word 'cash' could mean a lot of things, not just the money I might hold in my hands. The concept rather refers to its transferability than its financial identity. Anything from a mirror reflector to an actual Rama could be counted as cash.

'What kind of cash do you have in mind?' I ask.

The dealer approaches and rests on the pedaluxe's window with his only hand. He would have to bend down a lot for his head to come level with mine, so he just stands there and says:

'A thousand-dollar IC that's fully registered.'

It crosses my mind that I should have brought more with me. The goldsmith will no doubt ask for cash too. And perhaps I should just linger on the underground highway until a car or four-wheeled vehicle comes along and tag along behind it, to use its lights. But the dealer's Rama says, 'A piece of alpha quartz would also do, sir.'

Israfil must have read my mind and sent a pulse to the dealer's Rama, so now he's suggesting he accept an alpha quartz instead of an IC.

I reach for a five-carat piece of purple quartz and show it to the dealer. 'So I should present something of value to your majesty,' he says and walks to the desk he has placed between two silicon trees that have become a kind of makeshift office. Under the desk stands a wooden footstool, whilst on top of it is a mass of old cassette players, amplifiers, and subsonic tapes. He approaches the desk and retrieves three thousand-dollar ICs from a drawer, counts them in front of me, then throws them, along with the coin-shaped battery, at my feet.

'These ICs belong to the pre-pandemic period. They're sterilised, of course.'

Israfil takes a UV detector from under his feet and scans the quartz and the battery to make sure they aren't polluted. Then I put the gem in the palm of the dealer's hand.

'I've been keeping this for a long time,' I say. 'I didn't know it would ever be of use.'

'Whatever was useful yesterday will be useful tomorrow,' says the Rama with a mushroom cloud tattoo on his chest and takes two coated wires and hands them to Israfil.

'For connecting to the battery. Anytime.'

'Let's go, before it costs us more,' Israfil says.

On our way to Highway 8, Israfil connects the battery to the lamp, but it isn't charged and fails to turn on the light. We have given away an alpha quartz worth a thousand bucks for a battery that doesn't even hold any charge, and now we're looking at three years jail time if anyone arrests us with it.

'Even his Rama didn't know the battery had no charge,' says Israfil.

When a man hides his thoughts from his Rama, it can only mean one thing: that he is an agent of the state. State agents hold a frequency deflector, something that interrupts the brain's signals and enables them to hide their thoughts from their Ramas. A deflector consumes a lot of energy and is therefore too expensive for anyone other than government agents.

'Let's go back to the first gate,' I say.

'No,' says Israfil, 'Let's get a battery from your father. I know where he keeps them.'

My father's house is under the Highway 5. More than half of the population of Tehran now lives underground. The city has become a mirror of its pre-pandemic state. If you want a penthouse, with a view, you can simply buy a place on the minus forty-eighth floor. You can have any view you want: all the walls of the apartment are covered with screens that play views on request – timeless views of Pas-Qaleh and Dar Abad, or views from the ancestral towns or villages they come from. My father lives in one such apartment, his view being of Saqarisazan district in Rasht. He has never been there or seen it, himself, but he likes to play scenes of people coming and going in the market places and the shopkeepers taking afternoon naps. Sometimes he even inserts holograms of Erfan and me amongst the customers in the market. It might be a rainy morning, for instance, and we pass and sometimes stop at a window to stare into a shoe shop, while he is standing and watching us nostalgically. Sometimes he records such simulated scenes and sends them to us. I keep his videos on my searchband. Erfan never opens them, but I do and sometimes reply back with am emoji, something like an 'I love you' sign.

Sometimes in the videos we are standing together and are busy speaking – Erfan and me and him in one frame.

'Let's go,' I say, 'before he starts nagging about why I never visit him.'

Israfil stares at me for a moment, then lowers his head, and mumbles, 'You're afraid of the dark.'

I am indeed afraid of the dark, but I don't like being reminded about it. 'I'm also afraid of my father's actions,' I add.

As we reach the parking lot of my father's residential tower, I consider not going down, and sending Israfil to fetch the battery instead. I know that thinking about anything means sharing it with Israfil, and I wouldn't mind if he just went down of his own accord to get the battery without a single word. I don't feel like facing my father right now. Last time I saw him, we just fought. 'He's old now,' says Israfil. 'He hasn't got the energy for it anymore.'

'Tell me something good about him,' I say, 'something motivating for me to want to see him again.'

'One day,' he begins, 'when you were fourteen, you came home, to the house in Atisaz, where you still live. There was a dark circle round your eye. You'd been in a fight with someone and you never said who – not to me, Firouzeh, or your father. Firouzeh was concerned that you were setting a bad example for Erfan, so she kept interrogating you but you wouldn't say. You two quarreled for a while, then she called your father. When he arrived, he took me to another room to get to the bottom of it. I told him that you wouldn't say. Then he asked me to probe into your brain's wavelength and find out. I said that I could only synchronise with one person at a time. At that moment, he hugged me and said that from then onwards, I should be your Rama.'

'This scene is of sentimental value to you, not me,' I say. 'Tell me something that would matter to me.'

Israfil raises his hand, strokes the collagen shell over my face, and says, 'For one last moment, every datum of information his office held was in me, all his accounts and messages from clients. After that, I would have to start from scratch, and find it all again.'

His fingers seem to be caressing my mind and taking away my ability to resist. 'That night, I beat Erfan so hard that Firouzeh had to take him away to a villa in Siahkal for a whole month.'

Israfil opens the pedaluxe door and gets out, saying: 'If you don't want to come, I'll fetch the battery myself.'

'There's nothing in the past that connects us,' I say. 'We have nothing in common.'

Israfil is crossing the car park by this point, unable to hear me, but I'm sure he knows what I'm saying. I will have to take off my shell in the lobby locker room, disinfect it, and put it on again on my way out. I will have to wrap up the conversation in a way that wouldn't hurt my father's feelings.

'When you're a teenager, you don't understand the nature of your parents' work,' I say. 'All I knew was you were supposed to spy on me.'

Israfil is some distance away, but all these words must be stored somewhere in his memory already. The lobby attendant, who has a two-centimetre-thick plexiglass shield in front of the counter, asks for my name.

'Tell him "Arsanjani",' I say.

'Are you a relative of Mr Arsanjani?'

'Yes,' I reply, 'a relative.' I have visited my father's tower once or twice before. The lobby attendant isn't young or inexperienced, but he doesn't know all the residents. He sounds like a very polite stranger when he messages my father, then says, 'Mr Arsanjani would like to know, Love or Mysticism?'

'You sit upstairs and we sit downstairs,' I say.

The lobby attendant looks perplexed but repeats the phrase to my father, and then says, 'Insight or Method?'

I think for a moment, wanting to play it right and not make a mistake. My father is fond of such verbal games. 'Love or Mysticism' means: is it me, his love, or Erfan. But I should make sure my response is metaphorical. My response will determine the entire sequence of words that follow. Usually, I'd say Method. The journey means more to me than arrival. I often prefer to be a stylish player than a good one, someone known for their technique, admired and looked up to.

'Love should come with grace.'

Israfil takes my fingertips in his hands and says, 'Enough.'

The lobby assistant repeats my words and comes back with: 'He asks that you go in alone. Don't take your Rama with you.'

I look at Israfil. He closes his eyes, meaning he doesn't mind, saying, 'There's a lithium battery in a thermometer in the storeroom. It's been there for years and your father's forgotten about it. Firouzeh doesn't use it either.'

I take off my shell. I often weigh myself after taking it off to see how much water my skin has lost, but I am not in the mood for such trivialities now. I wash my hands in the locker room and throw my shell in a sterilising machine. By law every building must have a public locker room, where you can take off your clothes and put on sterile overalls, but my father's place has one for every apartment. All corridors and elevators are equipped with virus detectors and if your body temperature is over 39 degrees, no door opens for you, even if you are the owner and know all the passcodes by heart.

My father's locker room overalls are blue, a kind of blind blue – somehow joyless or soulless. The overalls are made of anti-virus fibres, but because it's a generic item, not meant to fit anyone, it fits no one, and it makes you feel like you've just been taken out of the nuthouse. When he opens the door, he hugs me. He hugs me without saying a word, his eyes glistening. He is always like this: all thunder and threat, then tears, then he throws you out of his house, swearing and cursing. He whispers in my ear, 'Mere austerity won't make you a lover; aspiration is needed indeed.'

The screens around the flat are off and just emitting a pale phosphorescent wash. My father is a few kilos overweight, and his custom-made clothes fail to hide it. I never understood how he got the money for such extravagant things – he always has money to spend on a ruby tie pin or a silver-nibbed fountain pen.

My father's in the habit of often thoughtlessly cursing Firouzeh, my stepmother, and often looks at me in the same way, meaning I should be grateful for everything he did for me, but it is the kind of behaviour that annoys me and led to Erfan running away from home. He has done good things as well, of course, like leaving the Atisaz apartment to me, and another place to Erfan – which he rented out while he lived in a farm in Chkam instead. He loved old cinema, and would occasionally recommend a bad movie: 'One should watch both good films and bad films,' he often says. 'If you only see the good ones, you stop knowing the difference between good and bad.' He used to play Mad Max movies and force us to watch them, though each time he would end up swearing at everything in them.

'I've missed you so much,' I say.

His scent fills my nostrils. He has been wearing different variations of Pierre Bourdon all these years, and I wondered how he still manages to find his favourite cologne in the market these days.

'I asked you not to bring Israfil, because I wanted to chat with you,' he explains.

'I'm in a hurry,' I say, 'I have to go to the bazaar to find a goldsmith.'

As I start this sentence, I know it won't lead anywhere good, but I don't have the time for his delusions right now, so I start towards the storeroom. He follows me, wearing his leather slippers and shouts, 'What do you want?'

'You've got a lithium battery in the storeroom,' I say.

He keeps shouting: 'You're thirty-five years old and can't get yourself a battery from a dealer.'

I try not to shout back at him, but my voice has risen. 'Well, you didn't raise me properly,' I say.

I go into the storeroom. It is full of 50-litre bottles of water, neatly piled up and fastened together with a metal strap. There is no sign of a thermometer. On the shelves, there are ceramic, bronze and wooden statuettes of elephants lined up in different sizes. I bend and look in among the well-arranged shelves and shout back: 'You had a thermometer here, right?'

My father comes in holding a metal box filled with all sorts of batteries. I stand up and wipe my pants. My father leans on one of the bottles and says: 'The world is going to get back to its former state one day. There will be no governments, no Ramas, no water. We're all going to die, but I'd rather die with a bunch of batteries in my hand.'

'That's how everyone feels out there,' I say, 'but not everyone can afford it.'

As I reach out to take one of the batteries, he grabs my hand. 'You know how a man like me dies?' he asks, then shuts his mouth, having set his trap. Any response will start a lengthy quarrel. So I just kiss him on the soft part of his cheek, and say, 'Few people in this world become a man like you.' My father is a smart man and can tell if I'm just flattering him, but my words seem to please him and he lets my hand loose. I inhale his perfume once again, then get out of there. In the locker room, I wait for my shell's sterilising process to complete. I think about calling Erfan and convincing him to invite us, my father and I, to his place. It would be good for all three of us, I think; we could talk about all the things that made Erfan cross and move to the north. On my searchband, I type 'dreaming of an elephant'.

A few more pages of information about the Ramas pop up, but then something funny draws my attention: it is claimed that if someone dreams about getting off an elephant and getting on another one, it means that he will go from serving one king to serving another king. 'Do you still dream about elephants?' I text Erfan. He hasn't seen my last few messages, and it's unclear when he's going to get this one.

By the time I reach the parking lot, Israfil has fallen asleep on the pedaluxe's driving seat. Ramas sleep when they have nothing to do, but their sleep is much deeper than that of humans. They cut off all contacts to the other Ramas when they sleep, and their bodies don't react to external stimuli. The only thing that wakes a Rama up is the sound produced at the frequency of its owner's voice. So I get in and start to pedal, in the dim glow cast from my flashlight onto the floor of the underground access level. The beam feels like a scalpel in the jerky hands of a surgeon who needs to cut through a patient's skin to reach the intestines but is too afraid of damaging something vital to go deep enough. Likewise, our speed feels insufficient if we are ever to reach the end of the highway. I pedal in silence, and the sound of the chain wheel rotating and halting with every turn is trancelike. Like a magic word uttered so frequently it has lost all meaning.

I finally make it out of the underground and reach the

surface. Tehran's summer light shines down on us, dispelling the narrow beam of my flashlight. I take out the battery and place it in Israfil's hands. If they catch a Rama with a battery or some other energy storage device, they will let him go, because the regulations don't apply to Ramas.

The first recorded contact with Ramas was in Southern India, where Eve is believed to have fallen and where the first piece of leaf she used to hide her private parts went on to generate huge forests.

This is how the official history goes: A woman saw a Rama and shouted, 'Uncle Rama! Uncle Rama!' finding the creatures so familial and amicable. It suited historians that first contact was made on a patch of paradise rather than, for instance, in the Lut or Gobi deserts. It made for a better metaphor – that these peaceful aliens had been given a name in a corner of paradise by a woman who said in Dravidian: 'How much he looks like my Uncle Rama!'

The largest number of Ramas to arrive in one go – 162 – was recorded on March 12, 2026, in the French region of Moselle near the *Centrale nucléaire de Cattenom*. Since then, there has been a prolonged legal dispute between Germany, France and Luxembourg over the ownership of this group, which took three years and two appeals before an A.R.C. union was finally founded with a budget of about four billion euros, of which all EU countries had a share. But just before the A.R.C. could unveil the first commercialised specimens, a Korean company released a cloned version of the Ramas onto the market. They had discovered Ramas' IQs were four hundred times higher than humans', with a very fast intersubjective transmission, and a 30 GigaHertz processing speed that was faster than any available supercomputers. This was both good and bad. Soon anti–Rama movements started to emerge all over the world, all wearing the same clothes and sporting the universal logo: three concentric circles. If they came across an unclaimed Rama on the street, they would beat him to death. Of course, they'd always get caught by the authorities because Ramas sent their video footage to the nearest Rama in the vicinity. But killing a Rama didn't come with a prison sentence attached; all you had to do was pay compensation to the Rama's owner. In fact, that was how many people got rid of their Ramas: they would throw them out of the house and wait for the police to appear with the corpse and collect the compensation.

As we leave Highway 8, everything seems like it's in the past, like my memories of the pre-pandemic period. Before those twelve long years of the shutdown. It is as if they have cut the bazaar out of the Tehran map and preserved it somewhere, only to then paste it back years later. There might be other locations like this – other than Evin and the bazaar; there might be other still-preserved locations in Tehran that haven't been replaced by the underground towers, but where are they, is the question. They're absent, at least, from all state channels and official information pages. Anything from the past is censored, any images that remind us of how we used to live in Tehran, and how much we cherished our lifestyles back then. As we reach Tekyeh-Dolat Alley, I have to wake Israfil. He hasn't transferred the goldsmith's address to my searchband. He opens his eyes and, for seconds, is surprised, not believing that such a place still exists on Earth. 'How long have I been asleep?' he asks.

'The usual,' I say, 'and now you should be at peace with everything in the world.'

Israfil frowns. He frowns like my father does. 'You had better see Erfan,' he says. 'Go to Kasma. Meet with him.'

'Let's get this connector first. Then we'll talk.'

I climb off the pedaluxe and Israfil follows me. There's no one in the street, nobody to buy or sell things to. No one to ask where our ambitious goldsmith might be. As we climb down the workshop's stairs, the muffled sound of a tonbak rises to meet us: at the bottom, the entrance forces me to step under a shower and walk through a puddle. In the back, seven men, both young and middle-aged, sit on stools with their backs to us, shirtless and in shorts, swaying to the rhythm of the drum, as if the music is guiding them in some collective project. They are, however, working in solitude, most of them filing and polishing, with two of them busy stone setting. The floor is covered with a chequered rubber matting so that the gold dust can be swept up more easily. None of the goldsmiths turns his head to us, so we can't see their faces. But one of them, with blond hair and light eyes, shouts, 'Tell your Rama to stay at the threshold. He's not allowed in here.'

The man tries to follow the drumbeat's rhythm as he speaks, but he fails and the others laugh. The tonbak player has wrapped a cloth round the drum to muffle the sound – he too is practically naked. No one is wearing a collagen shell in here, which is perhaps why they don't want any Rama to witness and record this. Nor do they ever turn round, so no one can identify them. Mushtaq seems to be the father or the head of the family. Such crafts are kept within families and passed down from father to son only, or at least remain in the family.

I pour a full glass of tea and sit down on a stool. I think about how long it's been since I've done anything on my own, with my own bare hands. The chores had always been done for me. Even using singular verbs and pronouns, and referring to myself like this, was a new thing for me. Israfil has always been there. I glance at the hand of the man drawing a soft file over a piece of gold and dispersing the invisible dust into the air with the other hand. He does this so unconsciously, it's as if he has no will of his own. A young man climbs down the stairs, starts towards the samovar and pours himself some tea. He has gel in his hair, wears torn jeans and a thick gold chain around his neck. The blond man from before speaks up, in time to the drumbeat: 'They're here for you, Mister Mushtaq.'

And the other goldsmiths echo: 'Aye Mister Mushtaq, Aye Mister Mushtaq.'

The young man, with the cup in his hand, pours the tea into the saucer then guzzles it down, as if this is part of his entering the office routine. 'We don't have custom-built,' he says, 'and don't take orders. And if someone's sent you here after a connector, he's made a mistake.'

'I think someone in Atisaz has bought a connector from you, and my Rama has found you.'

The young man sits down on one of the stools, like someone working in an old office who's forgotten where he's placed some of the old records and documents. 'Did he tell you how much?'

I glance back at the door under the stairs whose threshold is filled with Israfil's shadow – a short and desperate shadow. 'I've got a 10k IC quartz,' I reply.

The young man unfastens his searchband, places it on a goldsmiths table, then pushes it a little farther, and asks, 'Do you want a C-shaped connector or an L-shaped one?'

'A calibrated, C-shaped, ten to twelve.'

Mushtaq stands up, approaches one of the goldsmiths, picks up a C-shaped connector and brings it to me, holding it as if it's something of no value, as if he had no idea how many people depend on this piece now. 'It's worth eight grand, but I'll take ten from you. I'm telling you so you know.'

'No problem.'

He knows that he can sell it to me at any price he likes. He's probably bribed everyone on in the local committee, and he must've had his hand in the same bowl as all the big shots in government. He has all the confidence of someone who dines with an MP every day or spend his weekends in one of their villas.

'But you're going to tell your Rama that you bought this for twenty grand,' he adds, hoping to raise the price in our zone.

'He knows that I've only got ten grand,' I reply.

He swirls the connector between his fingers and says,

'Why do you feed your Ramas with this much information?' Then he fetches another connector, and says, 'So take two, for the same price.'

I can't figure out why he is doing this. I wonder how long it's been since I thought without my Rama's help. He has been clarifying situations for me.

'It's no problem,' I say.

'It *is* a problem,' he says, putting the two connectors in the palm of my hand. 'It's a big problem for you. If they arrest you with one connector, you can claim it's for personal use. But if they arrest you with two, it will be a crime against national security.'

My brain freezes; for a moment, I'm unable to understand anything – neither Mushtaq's words, nor why the workers seem to be singing, nor why I'm here at all. 'Then why are you giving me two?' I ask.

Patiently, Mushtaq fills another tea glass, sits down, and slowly sips it. The tonbak-player puts his drum away and all the singing and swaying workers go still, as if no swaying has ever taken place. 'I know you,' says Mushtaq. 'We've seen your photos before. Your father is a shareholder of B.P.A. With that much money, why should you be desperate for a tiny connector?'

Suddenly, everything feels like a trap, sprung especially for me. Someone has had to convince their Rama that a goldsmith could be found in the bazaar and made him share that info with Israfil. But why do all this? Just to extort my father?

'I don't live with my father,' I say, 'and I didn't live with him during the twelve pandemic years either.'

Mushtaq puts the narrow-waisted tea glass down on the desk, raises his shoulders and prepares himself for a long sermon. 'In the end, the rich will eat each other...' he starts, but then he regrets saying this and slouches on the stool again, 'Take the two connectors in exchange for the 10k IC quartz. Tell your Rama the extra connector is for your father, or anyone that matters to you. Articulate the price clearly. Everyone in your neighbourhood has a shortage.' Then he turns his back, implying that the deal is over and it's time to pay.

'How do you know where I live?'

'The moment a customer sets foot in the bazaar, everyone knows what he wants, where he's heading and where he comes from.' Mushtaq then opens a protective case, which until now I had thought was a fridge, and shows me an exclusive, 'over-excess' Rama inside, blindfolded, then closes it and says, 'We have these, too.' Then he points to the other workers and adds: 'And so do these, but they don't take them everywhere.'

I climb up the workshop stairs and see Israfil crouching in a corner under the rain and staring at the sky. He could have waited inside the pedaluxe and stayed dry, but instead he was huddling there on the stone pavement. I run towards the pedaluxe in order to stop my collagen shell from getting heavier with rainwater. Like a wet dog, Israfil shakes himself off before stepping aboard, only to say, 'Mister Farzam, you had better go to Kasma. Don't stay in Tehran.'

Israfil has never called me by my name before, except once – the first time my father told him to be my Rama. It's like signing a contract: the Rama says your name and this affirms his loyalty to you. I look up and ask, 'Is something wrong?'

Israfil keeps silent. As we reach the interchange of Highway 8, there is a roadblock and a long queue of electric cars and motorless vehicles in front of it, where the dealer and his Ramas were standing earlier. I look at Israfil and he shakes his head, meaning he has no idea what is going on. I place the two connectors and the battery my father had given me in his hand.

'You may have to swallow them,' I say.

'We don't do such things anymore,' he replies with a pride

and a confidence I haven't heard before. Then he presses the connectors into his tiny palm so firmly that, if he were on his own planet, I figure the battery might have been deformed, but on Earth and given this planet's gravity, Ramas have no real way of expressing their anger or power.

'I love you,' says Israfil, 'and always have.'

He utters these words softly and slowly. We are sat behind a self-driving electric vehicle that isn't budging. It's one of those multifunctional models that can travel over land or water or even through the air, one that doesn't need any integrated AI circuits. An impregnable military fortress with viability for many days. I begin to notice there are many 'cars' like this in the queue, which feels strange, because it isn't the sort of car many people can afford.

A few government agents start to patrol around the vehicle, checking underneath it with mirrors on sticks. Israfil is bending forward and looking at the sky through the windscreen, his head turning repeatedly. The agents are now pounding on the windows of the car in front, drawing their weapons and pointing them at the passengers, shouting at them to get out, but the occupants don't seem to move.

An explosion is heard in the distance, and black plumes of smoke are seen rising over the mountains north of the city. The dealer who sold me the uncharged battery, wearing the same unmarked collagen shell, runs towards the agents with a laser shotgun. From the authority in his voice, I can tell he ranks higher than the other agents. For a moment our eyes meet, but he doesn't care, and fires a warning shot into the air, yelling that they will shoot at their communication system if the occupants don't get out. Then he points at us and commands the agents to let us pass. Along with one or two other pedaluxes, we pass through the barricades, and it's clear that this is a serious operation taking place. The highway on the other side is quiet and as we pedal down it, we get closer and closer to the smoke rising from the mountain, still unable to tell what the source is. We turn into the underground highway, knowing we will have to pedal all the way to the driveway of our own complex. By the time we get there, we'll be alone and it will be nighttime.

I search for Erfan's number on my searchband to leave a message for him. I have replayed the message in my mind several times, and I don't know why but I feel like I've heard it in a movie and I'm worried he will think that too. So I don't send it.

'While you're recording this message, can you check if I have heard it somewhere before?' I ask Israfil.

Israfil takes his feet off the pedal and folds them under his body. 'Why don't you look it up with the searchband? It has better access to information than me.'

'Because I don't want to compare it with everyone else's data,' I explain. 'I just want to know if it's something Erfan and I might have heard before.'

'We weren't a very happy family,' I continue, 'merely a respectable one. We knew how to adjust our distances from each other so perfectly that we seemed to have been produced by a machine in the production line of a cream biscuit factory. Father and Firouzeh were the two sides of the biscuit. You and I made the cream in between them. I was a sugar-free, diet cream; you were a chocolate and nut cream. We regulated the distance between them, Erfan. And the distance has always been there, no matter how much we imagined we were filling in the distance with our gestures and mannerisms.'

I look at Israfil, expectantly. A faint smile plays on his lips, as he replies: 'It could be a line in a Coen brothers movie. It's in that style. But no, you haven't heard it in any movie.'

I send the message to Erfan and pedal faster so as to arrive at home in the last beam of sunset. As we enter the parking lot, it is dark and smells of smoke. None of the public lights of the complex are on, as nobody agrees to pay their share for the public charges. When we reach our door and put the key in the lock and turn it, I breathe a sigh of relief. If this connector works, everything in the house will get back to normal.

'Take this connector,' I say to Israfil, 'and install it while I am fixing the energy circuit.'

'I can't work for you any longer,' he says.

I get angry. 'You've been acting like this all afternoon. What's going on?'

I squat down next to him and hold his hand. 'Don't worry,' I say. 'You haven't done anything wrong. The goldsmith said there's a Rama in the complex that feeds them with information. It's not your fault.'

Israfil takes his hand out of mine, moves towards the terrace, and stares at the sky. There is nothing there, and he is too short to see down into the prison or that it's the prison that's on fire. Thick smoke is rising from the adjoining buildings. It's burning so furiously, it's as if someone has poured gasoline on everything in there. I think about those figures I used to watch every day, who are now running through the streets looking for weapons and like-minded people to let us live the way we want to.

With his finger, Israfil points to an emptiness in the sky and says: 'We are arriving.'

Note

1. In Islam, Israfil is the angel who blows the trumpet to signal the Day of Judgment. He is the oldest of four archangels in the Islamic tradition, along with Michael, Gabriel, and Azrael. He is commonly thought of as the counterpart of the Judeo-Christian archangel Raphael.

Tala and Mahtab

Porochista Khakpour

Khuzestan, 2053.

WE HAD COME TO the region in hopes of elders. We were looking to interview the eldest of elders, actually. Against all odds, in this village, in this previously glorious and now sometimes intentionally forgotten region of Iran, there were several women who had lived to 100 years or more. They said *or more* because no one was certain how old they were. This was the kind of place where no one was that sure of their birthdays, where no one was counting their years the way most do elsewhere. They had other concerns.

The wetlands were drying out, just like the rivers, everyone was telling us. They would point to the sky, so often a hazy yellow, on the brink of yet another dust storm. Rich in dust, low on water. For a long time, the region had been known for its resources, all the oil a country could lust after, land so fertile nearly any crop could flourish there. But even though this region had survived being on the frontlines in a deadly war, the destruction from that was nothing compared to the destruction from oil extraction, which is how the water was lost in the first place. Acres and acres of date orchards left in peril. Poisoned water from pesticides and pollution from sugar cane production. All the dead birds and fish. There are so many ways to destroy a water supply. Khuzestan knows this well. Dams and lagoons used to be part of the magic of this place. It was actually a place of beauty. Now it is known for having the worst air in the world, the most exploited natural resources, the least hope for a future – they kept telling us that. Every type of hell lives here now, whether flood or drought. There is no future, this is what we kept hearing. *You'll see*, they kept assuring, if you could call that assurance. *Stay here long enough, and you'll soon see.*

But we had other ideas.

The elders. Two of them had agreed to talk: a woman named Tala and another named Mahtab. They did not want their last names used. They claimed they were cousins, but several people said that was not true. Or at least not literal. Maybe since they had grown up next to each other all these years, in this same small town, same age, people had assumed they were blood. Maybe they had forgotten they weren't. They had, after all, been inseparable since birth.

They weren't amenable to outside translators, so we had to rely on a woman in town, an Iranian-American, who had spent the past decade living among the villagers. They said she was born in Iran and had spent most of her life in the States. Then, inexplicably, as she got to old age, she had moved to Iran in hopes she could die there. But she was still alive. Compared to the women we were interviewing, she seemed young, though in reality she was 75. They said another reason she looked young was because she had eaten all that good food in the West. In her lifetime, it had still been good. She never mentioned this herself and instead insisted it was because she had no children of her own.

Tala had had many children, eight or ten, she said, depending on whether you counted the two she lost early on. Mahtab had had none – doctors had said she was infertile, so she had given up soon after she had started – and so she had helped raise Tala's children. There was even one child who needed special attention thanks to some kind of learning disability – a sullen child who would get ganged up on by the others the most – and Mahtab rarely left that child's side. Her husband had died early in their marriage, so she always had room for guests, which meant that Tala's kids were often at her home as well.

They shared everything. Even their stories they told in tandem.

We spent many hours with them, mostly listening.

'So, what do you say to those who think the secret to a long life is not having kids, Tala?' We had a list of topics; we wanted them to trust us; we could not afford too much silence.

'Who says that?'

'Who knows, people sometimes imply it. Other oldest people on earth. Old women.'

Tala rolled her eyes, big cloudy eyes whose black looked almost bluish in a certain light. 'Maybe for some. I wouldn't know. Ask Mahtab.'

You rarely saw Mahtab's eyes, her face often in some kind of squint, eyes tucked in by layers of wrinkled brown skin, like an undone worn leather pouch that could still just barely conceal, contain, protect. But Mahtab smiled more than Tala and this was the first time I saw how wide that smile could go. 'I mean, yes, I am an example, but Tala is the opposite, so that means these things don't count for much.'

Tala waved us away, and it was only then that we saw the prayer beads she was gingerly fingering. 'God's will is God's will. What control do we have?'

Mahtab, again smiling, head tilted to the heavens, echoed: 'That's right. God's will is God's will.'

Later, Tala had more questions. 'Also, we cannot be as old as some of those oldest women. Certainly there are a few who are one hundred and twenty or so?'

'I heard in India, in the mountains, some are one hundred and fifty,' Mahtab suggested, all squints and smiles. 'Old men. Holy men. Only God knows.'

'Anyway. Would you like some tea? We don't make tea like we used to, with the beautiful old samovars. We are not allowed.' We didn't know how but suddenly the beads were gone from her hands. Tala was strangely quick, we were realising. She was instead offering us glass mugs, in a way that felt like a demand.

Mahtab's voice suddenly shifted into a new register, a deep brokenness, pottery cracked. It was hard to hear someone so old sound so desperate. 'The regulations are horrible. That alone should kill us faster. You've heard? Our bathing restrictions? Please tell them.'

Our translator explained that, thanks to the water scarcity in the region, there were now all kinds of laws that had to do with water usage. You could get fined if you showered longer than five minutes per person. Few families were allowed more than a gallon of water a day. You could receive a tax break if your usage was less than half of that. The government was growing desperate, especially as climate change continued to get worse. Their water crisis had now made international news.

We knew we had to steer the conversation back to why we were there. 'We wanted to talk about the events of your birth year. It's not lost on us that it was a remarkable year, of course.'

Tala and Mahtab looked at each other, faintly amused.

'We were born then, so what can we add to this discussion?' Tala said. 'We don't remember. What do babies know?'

'I can talk to you about the revolution,' Mahtab suggested. 'We were 25. Both recently married. We can tell you about that.'

The reporter signalled to the translator that we could turn off the recorder and take a break. We were directed outside, where other members of the family were keeping themselves busy – maybe to avoid us, we considered.

Over by picnic table full of food – rice, lentils, bread,

cheese, nuts, herbs – we discreetly asked about the women's education levels.

The translator seemed irked. 'They are educated. Of course. But that doesn't mean they are experts on 1953. They were born then. This is why they want to talk about the revolution. Which is not unrelated. But that's where the memories live.'

We explained that the docuseries was looking back at 100 years since 1953.

'I thought it was about the oldest women in Iran?'

'That too. I mean, the icon of 1953 was an old man.'

The translator looked at us with suspicion in her eyes. 'I think you should sit back and let them tell you what they want. Who knows how long they have? I used to be a journalist too. I let the stories take me where they wanted to. Of course, it was a different time then for journalists.'

'You've heard what has happened to our industry?'

The translator nodded vigorously. 'Indeed. So much so that I was surprised to see a live human sent here. Not that an AI could have done your job, but… maybe an AI could have done your job.' The translator flashed a quick knowing smile that we struggled to read.

'We are in a crisis.' We tried to put the truth plainly – an offering. We realised we'd been trying to win the translator over since we met her

It was no use.

The translator looked bored with that kind of candour. 'We said that for decades.'

'You are no longer a journalist.'

'I listened.' This time the translator put on a big smile. 'There are worse crises.'

'How do you survive now?'

'Being an old woman in Iran is not terribly expensive!' She was so amused, amused in the most bitter way. 'Now is it, Tala?'

Tala had either not heard or did not care to hear; she announced she needed a nap and Mahtab nodded in agreement. Apparently, they napped together, two cots side by side, outdoors in the summer heat.

The translator by then could read our minds, it seemed. We were beneath her, we felt that, but still she had a job to do, so she kept us in the loop. 'It won't be long. They imagine it's hours but at most they nap for half an hour. Then we have some tea and they start making preparations for dinner. Tala's daughter comes around to help make it, or else brings something over.'

We decided to sit and wait. The afternoon heat felt beyond oppressive. We'd been warned about it, so we were wearing light colors and linens, but it still shocked us. The translator told us that actually there was a nice breeze that day and that all week, the temperature had been lower than they'd anticipated, so everyone was very grateful and the crew was quite lucky.

'The project must be blessed if God spared you like this.' We hated the subtlety of that jagged tension in the translator's voice, the oscillating acridity designed to make anyone question if it was calculated or just her.

We nodded agreeably, always, but of course it was hard to imagine worse heat. We'd been told that in a few months the absolute worst would come, weather you could not leave your house for, not even for a few minutes. Dozens of people in the village would die, as they did every year, from bad luck, misfortune, random circumstance, or most often age. Tala and Mahtab had been a major consideration for the past couple of decades. They wouldn't leave their house for months. In that season, everyone feared another big earthquake striking in the middle of the day, knocking down buildings, and then what? What could possibly protect them from a sun like that? Everything would be over. Power outages were a regular problem across the country, but it was their unpredictability that caused the most chaos – hours here, seconds there, problem areas popping up here and there like bubbles in a boiling pot.

No one knew how long it would take for the lack of power to kill them, but they could imagine. It was a widespread fear.

'Something you will notice about Iran,' one of Tala's sons had said that first day, 'is that we are a nation of fears.'

We had replied that the same could be said of our country.

He nodded many times before he said very quietly, in a much lower register, 'Your country created some of our fears.'

It was our turn to nod.

Watching two old ladies nap outside on a hot afternoon was something. They wore matching nightgowns, plain white linen, and they wrapped themselves in white linen sheets. Our eyes could not stop lingering on how they slept holding hands, the fist made of their intertwined fingers dangling between the cots in that heavy, mostly still air.

'Yes, they sleep that way,' one of Tala's daughters said, a bit embarrassed. 'We don't know when it started. It makes sense, since they consider themselves sisters, or cousins at least.'

As we'd been told, their nap lasted almost exactly half an hour. Someone stirred and their fist came undone and the other rose too and soon they were joining Tala's daughter in the kitchen. Mahtab hummed, chopping vegetables. Tala and her daughter gently muttered to each other, making rice.

Tala suddenly turned to us. 'I want you to tell them about how we aren't going to survive. That each year it gets worse. That one of these years it will be too much.'

Mahtab laughed gently. 'They don't want to hear about that. They want to hear about us being old.'

'But that's it exactly. Our age makes it so that people don't care if we live. We have already lived enough. We are 30 years over the average. Most people don't even make it to the translator's age. So why should they care if we live, when we've already taken so much?'

'Had more than our share,' Mahtab said, that same old mournfulness in her shaking voice. 'That's what they think. That's why they don't want to hear —'

'I don't care!' Tala seemed irked, not with Mahtab but with us. 'I need you to tell your country to send us aid. We hear about your country and its factories and its airplanes and its ships and its wars. That's part of the reason why each year it gets hotter and hotter. Eventually we will all burn to death, even if we stay inside.'

'Tala, this is not what they want to hear,' Mahtab insisted, trying to make apologetic eye contact with us.

'It's true that it's not our focus,' we said. 'But we're willing to hear it all. We came all the way here, and you are giving your time. Maybe we can talk about it.'

'You'd have to make it fit into the story,' the translator said. 'Of these old ladies, the oldest we have, and instead of the secret to their success? Maybe talk about the threat to their success.'

'People don't like to hear old people are afraid of death,' Mahtab said. Again Mahtab's eye contact — the half-moon squint daring to open itself — was almost as apologetic as amused.

'This is true — I am in my late sixties, and I feel this myself,' Tala's daughter said. 'They prefer the old to be jolly, like they are grateful for their time and have no problem letting go.'

'But I want to live,' Tala said. 'I am not done.'

'Neither am I,' Mahtab echoed.

'I want to talk about the future, not the past, because I think forward. I believe I will exist in the future. I have to believe this.'

'I agree, Tala.'

'I think we will live to the same age,' Tala said. 'That's what everyone thinks.'

We wanted to say something and we didn't, of course.

Instead, Mahtab said: 'Yes, probably.'

'But I worry, because that likely means we will not die of natural causes but outside interference. Perhaps a horrible weather incident. More drought? Earthquake? Something crashing into us?'

'Tala is so negative.' Mahtab gently laughed. 'But I agree.'

'Mahtab worries too,' Tala said. 'She's not as open with outsiders.'

'We have had journalists come here before, and it's true that I am more shy,' Mahtab said.

'Journalists always come here wanting us to talk about certain things,' Tala said. 'Politics. Always politics. But we are worried about other things.'

'What are you most worried about?' we asked.

Tala pointed immediately to the ceiling, one long, bony finger gesturing to the heavens.

'God?'

Tala snorted, looking a bit angry. 'Why would God cause worry? God is the opposite of worry. No.'

'Then what?'

Tala pointed again. 'What else? The sun.'

Mahtab nodded. 'It's true. What else?'

'Do they know about 2021?' Tala turned to the translator. 'I am too tired to get into it all, but hopefully they know.'

Our blank stares probably said it all.

The translator turned wearily to us. 'Like me, in 2021 you were probably still preoccupied with the pandemic,' the translator began. 'But I remember it on the news even from America. There were huge uprisings here in Khuzestan. In the summer after Raisi's election. For two weeks Because of the drought. Water was running out and Tehran didn't care. So young men especially took to the streets. The local economy was already in trouble. No one had much to lose.'

'So much so that Raisi later gave his address from the local mosque here, in Khorramshahr!' Tala added. 'Suddenly Khuzestan mattered.'

'Or so they had to pretend,' Mahtab said. 'They hadn't seen protests like that since the revolution. "The Uprising of the Thirsty" it was called. They were all yelling, 'I am thirsty!"

'Of course, this was before 2022, when the Mahsa Jina Amini protests happened.'

'We have so much of Iran's natural resources, and yet so much poverty,' the translator explained. 'Oil was even discovered here in the early days of the twentieth century! This province has most of the country's oil and gas. And yet you would not know it.'

'It's awful,' Mahtab said.

'And almost half of the province is in poverty. The climate only threatens us more. The dust storms! My God. And now they say the solar storms. That will get us certainly. So the only thing I fear is the sun.' Tala looked up, flinching, as she said the word.

'We have five rivers, and they still dump waste into them, so we can't get drinkable water,' Mahtab explained. 'When we bought that filter you see there, the whole village was coming over. We eventually had to charge them.'

'When the young men of the village get angry again, just watch, there will be no next time. It's been happening for years. They will spare nothing. If we're going to die anyway, let's make it quick!' Tala laughed.

At dinner, the conversation again turned to our intent.

'What is the point of all this, anyway? Like the translator, will you one day just move here and become one of us? You Iranians in America keep coming here, now that travel has become easier these last few decades. You always say you will move, like it's a threat.' Tala looked amused at that, a hint of laughter in her throat.

'I would never leave America, if I had the choice,' Mahtab said.

'The Karoun River is full of islands. Dozens of islands. Maybe you in America think that is nice. Islands are for vacations. But islands for us come when the water level is dropping. And then the wildfires on the islands. Imagine. Crisis on crisis.'

'Everyone here has had this on their minds for decades now,' Mahtab said. 'So you'll excuse Tala.'

That did it: Tala pounded her first on the table. She was surprisingly strong; the table shuddered in response. 'Don't excuse me! Stop asking us about politics and the past. Look around.'

We did just that. We looked around. And we let the translator guide us away to our quarters.

Her words echoed in our ears as we went to sleep that night. We did not sleep well. Every few hours we would wake with a start, sure an earthquake had hit. Something about the ground did not feel stable in this village in Khuzestan, but the translator thought it was just nerves when we told her the next day. She wondered if we startled easily.

'Then again, ancient provinces have their own vibrations and frequencies,' she said. 'Maybe you are more connected to the land than you think.'

We tried our questions about the past again, but Tala and Mahtab only had a few topics they wanted to speak about.

'You have to understand, part of our being old, what you are interested in, is that we know we have limited time, so we must speak on issues that matter,' Mahtab said. 'Tomorrow matters to us, not yesterday.'

Tala refused to rationalise. She would often just respond with silence, her finger – sometimes still wrapped in prayer beads – always pointed upward at the one thing she feared.

On one of our last mornings, we woke up to what we thought was dawn, but it was actually 9am. The sky was orange, in a way we assumed might be early light, but the smell of smoke soon gave us our answer. The trees trembled chaotically – not from the breeze, but from the violent whiplash of the burning air.

We were not sure what to do. The rest of the crew were already out getting help with the translator.

We walked around the premises and stopped only when we saw Tala, hands on her hips at the border of the property, looking the fire in the eye.

'Tala, the smoke isn't good for you!' we called out to her.

'See? You finally see what I was speaking about!' she called back, grinning and waving at the sky.

We nodded. 'Yes, yes. It's terrible.'

She shrugged. 'It's our life. Next week it will happen again.'

We nodded. 'Let's go back inside. Mahtab is inside too. This smoke is bad for you.'

But she didn't listen. Tala stood there so still, like she was possessed, a tiny black shadow among lashes of orange and brown and black. We couldn't make out her prayer beads, but we suspected they were with her, she was so entranced in some otherworldly showdown. How she was breathing with all that, we did not know, except that maybe she was used to it. But if she was, wouldn't that have compromised her health? In what world does an ancient woman stand in the middle of a firestorm, like a defiant teacher facing an unruly classroom? We kept worrying she was in some kind of shock, she was so still, but no one else seemed to panic about it.

Eventually it got too much for us – our lungs were burning, our coughs layering over each other like a mad chorus of wild dogs barking, no rhyme or reason, until our bodies began to convulse and our coughs morphed into shouts and then cries for help – and so we rushed inside, inside without her.

Safety, or something close. We caught our breath. The air without smoke felt as nourishing as food.

Mahtab was at the window, watching calmly, a bit too calmly. Watching Tala watch.

'I wish she'd come back inside,' we said. 'The smoke can't be good for her.'

Mahtab shook her head. 'She knows. She does this every time.'

'It doesn't make her sick?'

'It does. A bit. But she says this is how it is meant to be.

She says if the plants and little animals are dying by fire, then she can at least bear witness.'

We nodded. 'What do you think, Mahtab?'

Mahtab paused for so long, we worried she had forgotten we were there. Her eyes were wet with something that could have been tears or else irritation from the smoke, which every minute seemed to intensify for us, even indoors. This would be a bigger crisis than we knew at that very moment, like so many crises, when you are unknowingly on the cusp of never returning. But ultimately Mahtab spoke, slowly and deliberately, the only words we remembered well from that terrible day: 'I think one day there will be one too many, and there will be nothing more for us to watch. Then someone else will. Until there are no more.'

We weren't sure if she meant nothing more to burn or no one left to witness.

Afterword

On 16 September 2022, Mahsa Amini died in hospital from her wounds after being arrested for not wearing her hijab properly. Her death sparked nationwide protests and the Woman, Life, Freedom movement – and, later down the line, it also sparked the idea for this anthology. We wanted to help Iranian voices be heard, as a way to be a part of, a continuation of, this ongoing struggle for human rights in Iran. As writers who were both involved in creative projects in English, and both engaged with speculative fiction, we naturally had the impetus to make an anthology of Iranian science fiction.

As second-generation immigrants, it only makes sense to us that our creative concerns reach out to where the political and the personal intersect. To immigrants, history isn't something that happened. It's something alive and present, that shapes our lives. If not for the Iranian Revolution or the Iran-Iraq war, our parents and grandparents might never have left Iran. Their lives would now have a different shape and, consequently, so would ours. The Iranian diaspora, with its strong ties to the families left inside the country, only exists because of the forces that have displaced the population. As science fiction writers ourselves, but also as people who understand that the past shapes the future, that history is a crucial part of our present – and that the present is a crucial part of our future – we decided to put together a science fiction anthology, where the ramifications of the 1953 coup could be explored into the distant future.

The past is a recurrent theme in the anthology you hold in your hands. Things that have been buried need to be properly put to rest or they will rise again – they may literally rise, as the undead body of Mosaddegh in 'For Malileh'; or the ground may sink and reveal the bones of old Tehran, unveiling secrets that were supposed to stay below ground, as in 'The Tomb'. In both stories, the past needs to be dealt with, and the truth of the 1953 coup needs to be addressed, before we can move forward. People who were silenced, by force, or by being dismissed as mad or unreliable, are the holders of a truth that needs uncovering. The importance of not only knowing the past, but also defending the truth of what happened, and giving it its proper dues, is central to these stories.

Another central theme is energy – more precisely, oil. A defining feature of Iran is its natural resources. One cannot talk about the coup, or about Iran's history, without talking about oil. It's what motivated foreign interference in Iranian politics, and it's the lens through which the international stage still, to this day, views Iran. 'Oil', the very first piece of the anthology, sets the tone. Oil is overwhelming, ever-present, impossible to forget, until it becomes a defining feature of people's lives, 'shiny and sticky, black and thick', sticking to people without them being able to get rid of it. This obsession isn't a choice. This constant worry happens because oil has defined Iran's international relationships for so long. As a country, if you're told only your oil matters, then maybe that's all you can think about when you think about yourself. In 'The Milkman of Xijing Ping Town', people kill for oil, people are killed for oil, people drown in oil. There is a bleak absurdity to these stories, where trying to define yourself through this sole resource ultimately ends in failure. Oil doesn't bring riches to the Iranian people, even though it may promise riches. It only brings heartbreak.

Energy, and the fight for it, leads us into another concern: the cyclical nature of revolution. 'The Blaze of Abadan' is an example of a story where all three themes intersect. Energy – in this case, the use of nuclear energy – is once again central. Energy affects people's lives. People are the ones who will suffer from economic change and the shift to different energy sources, as people now suffer from international sanctions. Thus energy becomes the catalyst for violence. The blaze in Abadan echoes the blaze of the Cinema Rex fire in 1978, a terrorist attack that led, in part, to the Iranian Revolution of 1979. These two fires brought change, in the fictional and the real world, but we are never sure, as readers, whether change will be for the better. Similarly, in 'Eye for an Eye', it's sometimes hard to know whether the cycle has been broken or simply continued with different players. Are the women who punish the men who have harmed them justified? Is their regime fairer? The authors don't judge – they set out their worlds and let readers decide.

Situations are reversed, from monarchy to democracy, from the rule of the mullahs to a republican rule, but the violent patterns remain. For a country that underwent a revolution to get rid of the Shah's oppressive regime, and that then suffered the oppressive regime of the mullahs, this is a pressing concern – does history always repeat itself, with revolution being only one part of its natural cycle, or can we hope for a better world? For an end to this cycle? 'A Suspended Spectre in the Tehran Sky' is very aware of this pattern, and weaves it into the fabric of the story itself. Whatever the cause, there is always a man suspended in the sky, and he is always falling. This is a wound struggling to heal – but it is also a repeated violence. Across each cycle of revolution, a brutality is happening on the street outside the window, but it always fails to save the man from falling.

Yet the story ends on a hopeful note. The narrator, heading upstairs, wonders if, at last, the man will be gone – if he will be at peace, no longer suspended. And that's something we'd like to draw attention to: how many of these stories are hopeful in the face of impossible odds. For despite being ostensibly about the past, what all these stories reach towards, as most science fiction does, is the future.

A lot of stories end on the cusp of something. 'Staring into the Void' ends just as its narrator steps through a portal into the unknown. 'Due Date' ends with the return of the Ramas, strange aliens that sit at the intersection between biology and tech, with one of them pointing towards the sky and announcing 'We are arriving.' This is a deeply Iranian storytelling technique: stopping just before the crucial moment. Readers don't get the easy answer of a clean resolution, with the exact consequences set out before them. The future remains uncertain. Readers can only infer, from what the story has given them so far, what might happen. This is also a component of hope. Hope is born of uncertainty – there is no need for hope if we're confident there'll be a happy ending. We only need it if we don't know what's on the horizon, and yet are willing to step forward anyway. As Javid tells us about the temporal voids in 'Staring into the Void': 'When you enter one, you don't know where you'll end up afterwards – you don't know if you'll be able to get out of it or not. But there's only one way to find out where it will take you: by entering it.'

This tension between past and future – acknowledging what happened but looking forward, bearing witness to the past but considering what the future holds – is well expressed in 'Tala & Mahtab', the closing piece of the anthology. Tala and Mahtab are the oldest women in Iran, but they don't want to play the interviewers' game and reminisce. 'I want to talk about the future, not the past, because I think forward. I believe I will exist in the future. I have to believe this.' They bear witness to what happened and reflect upon it, how it affected them and their country, but ultimately, they are interested in what happens next.

What happens next? This afterword is being written in

June 2025, mere days after Israel and the US launched unprovoked strikes against Iran. Three years after we first conceived of it, this anthology is as urgent as it was at its inception. It's been a long path to publication, from finding a publisher that would take on the project, to contacting the authors, all the way to ensuring we had security measures in place to protect the writers and translators. After years of work, it's heartbreaking to see ignorance of Iran's political history, and wilful ignorance of the experts' reports on Iran's nuclear energy, being weaponised to justify these attacks. This anthology cannot possibly respond to the current crisis so quickly, but hopefully it can give readers a much clearer sense of Iran's history, and a glimpse into the richness and creativity of Iranian culture – of what might be lost if the US and Israel engage in a war of aggression.

As editors, we hope this anthology lets Iranian voices be heard outside of imposed, often unhelpful, mainstream narratives. Mixed-heritage children learn to be bridges between cultures and identities. At times, we may, like Roshan in 'The Blaze of Abadan', think, 'I'm too American for the Iranians, like I'm too Iranian for the Americans.' Or too British to be Iranian, too Iranian to be British. But this intersectional identity is also a gift, as an understanding of both cultures can help bring them closer.

Ultimately, this is what we hope this anthology can be – a chance to bear witness, and a bridge, and a plea to keep the future hopeful.

Peter Adrian Behravesh & Rebecca Zahabi,
June 2025

About the Contributors

Alireza Abiz is a multi-award-winning Iranian poet, translator, and scholar with a PhD in Creative Writing from Newcastle University. He has published six poetry collections in Persian, translated several major poets into Persian, and authored a key study on censorship in post-revolutionary Iran. Translations of his own work have appeared in more than a dozen languages. A selection of his poetry in English translation, *The Kindly Interrogator,* was published by Shearsman in 2021. Based in London, he co-founded MAHA, edits literary podcasts, and serves on the Poetry Translation Centre's board.

Fereshteh Ahmadi (b. 1972) is a novelist, short story writer, literary critic and editor. Her first novel, *The Fairy of Forgetfulness* (2007) was a finalist of the Mehregan Award and the Rouzi-Rouzegari Awards for the Bookseller's Choice of the Best Novel. Her first collection of short stories, *Everyone's Sarah* (2004) featured 'Television', which was selected by the Hooshang Golshiri Foundation as one of the best short stories of the year. Her collections since include *Hyperthermia* (2013) and *Domestic Monsters* (2016). In 2019, she edited *The Book of Tehran* for Comma Press.

Peter Adrian Behravesh is an Iranian-American musician, writer, editor, audio producer, and narrator. For these endeavours, he has won the Miller and British Fantasy Awards and has been nominated for the Hugo, Ignyte, and Aurora Awards. His interactive novel, *Heavens' Revolution: A Lion Among the Cypress,* is available from Choice of Games, and his essay, 'Pearls from a

Dark Cloud: Monsters in Persian Myth', appears in the *OUP Handbook of Monsters in Classical Myth*. When he isn't crafting, crooning, or consuming stories, Peter can often be found hurtling down a mountain, sipping English Breakfast, and sharpening his Farsi. You can read his sporadic ramblings at peteradrianbehravesh.com, or on Bluesky @behravesh.

Caroline Croskery is an American Persian-to-English translator. She holds a Bachelor's Degree in Iranian Studies from the University of California, and has worked as a language teacher, translator, interpreter and voiceover actor. Caroline lived in Iran for thirteen years between 1985 and 1998, where she taught English and also translated and dubbed Iranian feature films into English. After returning to the US, she began a career as a court interpreter and Persian-to-English translator. Works she has translated include many titles by Houshang Moradi Kermani, including his latest novel *You're No Stranger Here*, as audiobook as well as hardcopy. She is now a cardiac sonographer and lives in Monterey, California.

Farzaneh Doosti is a professor of English at IAU, Central Tehran, and bilingual translator. Her interests include interdisciplinary and comparative studies, semiotics, narratology, diaspora studies, and Persian literature. She is the founder and Editor-in-Chief of *Parsagon: The Persian Literature Review*. She has won awards at the Tajrobeh Theater Festival (2008), Iran International Festival of University Theater (2008 and 2009), the Book Criticism Festival (2009), and the Abolhassan Najafi Award for Literary Translation (2021). She has translated a number of works by Mohammad Tolouei.

Ebrahim Farokh is a writer.

Behzad Ghadimi is an Iranian-Australian writer, born in 1983 in Tehran, and author of four novels, including *The Services of Damascus Monster-Making Machine* (2019), and *The*

Doomed Voyage of the Silver Axe (2020), both of which were shortlisted for a Noofe Award for Best Persian Speculative Fiction Novel. His short stories and novellas have won the Afsaneha Award and two Persian Speculative Fiction Awards. He won Paranthes's Best Speculative Fiction Book Award for his book, *Band of Daevas,* in 2023.

Navid Hamzavi has a Masters degree in Cultural and Critical Studies from Birkbeck, University of London. His works of fiction include the collections *Rag-and-Bone Man* (2010), *London, City of Red* (2016), which was banned at the Tehran International Book Fair, and the chapbook *Body: A Triptych* (Exiled Writers, 2021). Navid has read at various festivals in the UK and seen his stories published in *Ambit, Stand,* and *Critical Muslim.*

Naseem Jamnia is the Judith A. Markowitz Award-winning and Astounding Award-nominated author of *The Bruising of Qilwa,* a fantasy novella introducing their queernormative, Persian-inspired world, which was a finalist for the Crawford, Locus, and World Fantasy awards. Their middle grade horror debut, *The Glade,* following an Iranian American protagonist, was published this year by Aladdin. A Persian-Chicagoan, child to Iranian immigrants, community educator, and pro-library activist, Naseem lives outside Reno, Nevada, in the US, with their husband and four furred creatures. Find out more and join their newsletter at naseemwrites.com.

Porochista Khakpour is the author of five acclaimed books (three novels, a memoir, and an essay collection). Her other writing has appeared in *The New York Times, The Los Angeles Times, The Washington Post, The Wall Street Journal, The Atlantic, Esquire, Bookforum, Elle,* and many others. Among her many fellowships is an NEA award, as well residencies at Civitella Ranieri, MacDowell, Yaddo, Ucross, VCCA, and more. She is a contributing editor at *Evergreen Review*. For more info: www. porochistakhakpour.com

Nasim Marashi (b. 1984) is a journalist, writer and scriptwriter. She won the Premier Prix in the Bayhaqi Story Prize (2014) for the short story 'Nakhjir', and the Premier Prix in Tehran Story Prize (2015) for the short story 'Rood'. Her novel *Fall is the Last Season of the Year* (2015) was shortlisted for the Best Novel of the Year in the 8th Jalal-e Al-e-Ahmad Prize, and has been translated into Italian (Ponte33). She co-wrote the feature film *Avalanche* (2015), and wrote the short movie 'Haven' (2015), and the documentary *20th Circuit Suspects* (2017).

poupeh missaghi is the translator of, most recently, *Boys of Love* (Ghazi Rabihavi) and *In the Streets of Tehran* (Nila), both from Persian. Her own books include *Sound Museum* and *trans(re) lating house one*. She is assistant professor of literary arts and studies at the University of Denver.

Susan Niazi has a Masters degree in Translation Studies from the University of York and is currently completing her PhD in Humanities (on the reception of literary translation in modern Iran). Her English-to-Persian translations include Bertrand Russell's *In Praise of Idleness* (Kalagh, 2013). One of her Persian-to-English translations featured in *Shades of Truth: Iranian Short Fiction of the New Generation in Translation* (2019) and Comma's *The Book of Tehran* (2019).

Jim Preacher is a translator living in the UK.

Mohammad Tolouei (b. 1979) is a storywriter and playwright. He has published three short story collections: *I'm Not Janette* (for which he received the Golshiri Award in 2012), *Lessons By Father* (2014), and *Seven Domes* (2018), as well as three novels: *Fair Wind's Prey* (2007), *Anatomy of Depression* (which won multiple awards in 2017), and *Encyclopaedia of Dreams* (also published in Italian). In 2016, he was a finalist of the Chehel Literary Award for writers under 40.

Sholeh Wolpé is an Iranian-American writer, whose literary work includes seven collections of poetry, several plays, five books of translations and three collections, as well as texts and librettos for the choir and opera. Her most recent works include *The Invisible Sun – Attar* (Harper Collins, 2025), *Abaco de Perdida* (Visor Libros, 2025), and *Abacus of Loss: A Memoir in Verse* (University of Arkansas Press, 2022). She is the Writer-in-Residence at the University of California, Irvine (UCI), and the poetry editor at *The Markaz Review*. She presently divides her time between California and Barcelona.

Behnam Yousefpour studied filmmaking at the Iranian Youth Cinema Society, before taking a mechanical engineering degree at the Babol Noshirvani University of Technology (NIT). He has written and/or directed seventeen short and feature-length films and documentaries. He also studied creative writing and was taught by the feminist author, translator and poet, Shiva Arastouei, who went on to be an abiding influence on his work, until she tragically took her own life in May, 2025. Yousefpour has published one novel, *It's Exactly Midnight Now*, as well as numerous short stories.

Rebecca Zahabi is a British-Iranian writer, who grew up in France. Her short stories have appeared in various magazines, including *The Magazine of Fantasy & Science Fiction*, *Infinite Worlds*, and *PodCastle*. Her debut adult novel, *The Collarbound* (Gollancz, 2022), made it to the top ten *Sunday Times* bestseller list. Aside from writing traditional fiction, she also writes for video games. You can find her on Substack at rebeccazahabi. substack.com or on her website.